ACCLAIM

AIREL

"It takes rare talent for a man to write a novel from a male POV and have it published to great critical and commercial acclaim. But it takes a miracle for that same male, or in this case males, to write a novel from the POV of a teenage girl and have it turn out as incredibly as did the new StoneHouse YA by Aaron Patterson and Chris White, Airel. From the first sentence, I felt compelled to dive into this young woman's story and just as importantly, I felt like I personally knew her, which means I laughed, stressed and cried right along with her. A beautifully written and crafted fiction about teenage innocence, faith, loss and love. A must read for teens and adults alike."

—*Vincent Zandri, International Bestselling Author of The Remains, The Innocent, and Concrete Pearl.*

I am happy to say that this novel is one of my favorites of its kind. I never thought I could read a novel like this and be so swept away! I am always willing to try new books, but I usually steer clear of this kind of novel. Not anymore! Not when I can be so engrossed into the character's story, like I was with the beautiful Airel, that before I know, it's over. I kept turning the pages , wanting to, no-NEEDING, to know what was going to happen next.

—*Molly Edwards, Willow Spring, NC*

SWEET DREAMS

"Sweet Dreams was a book I read in 2 days. I truly enjoyed the read. It kept me wanting to know more. I'm looking forward to Part 2 of the WJA Trilogy!"

—*Sharon Adams, Novi, MI*

"Suspense, thriller with a perfect ending, leaving me wanting more. An on the edge of your seat, all night read. I most certainly will be reading "Dream On.""

—*Sheri Wilkinson, Sandwich, IL*

"New authors come and go every day. Very few come on the scene with the ability to weave a tale that will make you sad to reach the end, longing for more. At a time when the world needs a real hero, Patterson delivers big with the WJA's Mark Appleton—an unlikely hero for the 21st century."

—*The Joe Show*

"Aaron Patterson spins a good tale and does it well."

—*W.P.*

"*SWEET DREAMS* is packed with action, suspense, romance, betrayal, death, and mystery."

—*Drew Maples, author of "28 Yards from Safety"*

DREAM ON

"Once again, Aaron Patterson has made a home run!
'Dream On' is a wonderful read from cover to cover! I am
now anxiously awaiting his next book "In Your Dreams."
I originally purchased his first book by mistake, and
was pleasantly surprised at how much I enjoyed it... so
now I'm hooked! Aaron has got to start writing faster!!!
Although his books are definitely worth the wait! Bet'cha
can't read just one! This guy has real talent for writing and
keeping the suspense growing... the worst part about the
book is the last page... I hated it to stop!"

—Ruth P. Charlotte, NC

"After reading Patterson's first novel, 'Sweet Dreams,'
I was really looking forward to reading 'Dream On.'
This book was amazing. I couldn't put it down. If you're
looking for an exciting read, read this book."

—Paul Carson, Boise, ID

"I read the first book by Aaron Patterson (Sweet
Dreams) and was very anxious for this sequel. I was not
disappointed. This book kept me guessing with every
page turn. It's very well written and I really enjoyed the
technology employed, which makes it just a bit futuristic
without being over done. This was a fantastic suspenseful
thriller that kept me guessing throughout the entire book.
Mr. Patterson has become my favorite fiction writer."

—Donna H. Boise, ID

"This is the second book of Aaron's I have read and I have to say he is a very talented writer!!! I read this book in under 12 hrs; it was so good I couldn't put it down. He managed to surprise me with a twist that I did not expect! It is filled with suspense and keeps you guessing throughout. I will be suggesting this book to everyone I know..."

—*Amanda Garner, Oklahoma*

Aaron Patterson
IN YOUR DREAMS
Book three in the WJA Series

StoneHouse Ink 2011
StoneHouse Ink
Boise, ID 83713
http://www.stonehouseink.net

First eBook Edition: 2011
First Paperback Edition: 2011
ISBN: 978-0982770597

In Your Dreams: a novel/by Aaron Patterson
Cover design by Fuji Aamabreorn

Published in the United States of America
StoneHouse Ink

Also by Aaron Patterson

Sweet Dreams (Book 1)

Dream On (Book 2)

In your Dreams (Book 3)

Airel

Michael (coming soon)

19 (Digital Short)

The Craigslist Killer (Digital Short)

The eBook on eBooks (Digital Short)

This is the third book in the Mark Appleton series. If you have not read the first two books, please do so in order not to miss some key elements. Sweet Dreams *is the first in the series and* Dream On *is the second. You can find them at www.stonehouseink.net, at your local bookstore, or as an eBook online.*

Aaron Patterson

IN YOUR DREAMS

~ The Perception of Truth ~

For you dear reader,
Thanks for believing

CHAPTER ONE

2012 B.C., Havilah, Arabia

KREIOS RAN FULL TILT through the dense forest, his long robe fluttering behind him like a frightened bird. He could hear the creatures behind him cursing and spitting in fury as they searched for him in the darkness.

Kreios was a big man with strong arms, chest, and legs. He did not hesitate as he leaped over a dead log in his path. In spite of his size, he was fast and moved through the forest without a sound.

The warm night sky loomed overhead, and a fat, low-hanging moon looked on with indifference. Kreios clutched a book in his left arm and ducked under a branch, avoiding a head wound. The two *things* behind him crashed through the underbrush like unskilled hunters. Kreios ran without looking back. He knew that he must keep the book safe at all costs, even if it meant his life.

A howl erupted from his flank, and Kreios dove for cover under a huge willow tree root. He calmed his breathing, tucked the leather bound book tighter under his robe, pulled the hood up over his blond hair, and curled up in a ball.

He waited.

A snort and the footsteps of the two attackers came close to his hiding spot; nevertheless, he was not discovered. Two hours passed, and the beasts gave up their hunt and moved out, heading west, back to their camp. The Seer would be very angry with them and might even take their lives because of their failure. Kreios did not mind, he hoped they would die and leave him with one less of their kind to kill.

Working his hand free, he removed the book and looked at it with awe and wonder. Inside, words glimmered, and though he read it every night, he was surprised to find that in the morning the words would disappear. However, by just a thought, they would reappear and shimmer like diamonds.

The book had his name on the cover and contained the complete history of his kind and their fall. In the wrong hands, it would mean death and enslavement. Climbing to his feet, he crossed the small creek and ran north. He had escaped this time, but he had many more battles to fight before the book would be safe.

Present day, Manhattan, New York

ALONE, LYING IN A hospital bed, a man breathed

through a tube and thought of how he came to be here. He was smart; in fact, he was a genius by the world's standards. Yet here he was, alone, with no visitors, and not even his mother had come by to see him.

He could still see the flash of the gun barrel as two shots rang out and feel the fire as the bullets hit him in the chest. He was a lucky guy, or so his doctor told him, but he didn't feel lucky. He felt abandoned, betrayed, and his anger boiled over like a pot on a hot burner.

Mooch hated the feel of the feeding tube. The hoses and wires made him feel like he was in a sci-fi movie, like he had been abducted by aliens and was about to be experimented on. How could they leave him to die? If they really were his friends, they would have helped him, but see what he received in return?

His thoughts brought Kirk Weston to the front. He could see his stupid face looking down at him. He was the reason Mooch was in this mess; he was the one who held control over him, and just look at what he did. *Here I am, shot up, left for dead, and alone!*

"You are not alone, not anymore. Invite me in, and you will have your revenge."

"Who are you?" Mooch could feel something tickle the back of his mind. It was like an old friend, a chum whom you thought you would never see again, but when you needed someone to confide in, here he was.

"I am whatever you want me to be. I am fear, I am desire, I am need, and I am the power of the most high. Trust me, and you will not die!"

Mooch opened his mind and soul for the second time in his life and felt a warm, wonderful wave of beauty fill him. He felt stronger, and his chest didn't hurt anymore. "Thank you—thank you for staying with me."

Mooch talked aloud in an empty room on the third floor of a second-rate hospital in Manhattan. The ambulance had received the call, and when they got on scene, they found Mooch alone in his basement, bleeding from two gunshot wounds to the chest. They tried to revive him, but could not get a pulse. On the way to the hospital, he jerked and somehow regained a heartbeat.

Sometimes weird things happened. For some, it just wasn't their time to die.

DO YOU WANT TO die?

It may seem like a simple question with an even simpler answer. Of course I don't want to die, who would? But then again, with the question comes an assumption that one may want to consider before jumping too quickly. I did want to die at times; in fact, I almost died when I was buried alive by a terrorist named the Red Dog.

I made it out, and if I told you how I did, you would call me crazy—looney, bonkers—and maybe you'd be right. I still didn't know what happened, and how I killed the Red Dog was even weirder. Light, hot white light came from my hands and chest like a weapon.

Whatever it was, it made me think about my life and where it was going. Was I a danger to K and Sam? Could I blow up and kill them as well as others around me? This question haunted my dreams, and now, as I pondered the question of death, the once simple answer did not seem so simple after all.

K, my beautiful wife and best friend. Because of me she had been put through so much: a kidnapping and so many long nights alone when I should have been home instead of out killing someone. But what was a guy to do? I was a contract killer—well, not really. I was an assassin for the World Justice Agency. The WJA.

The WJA was a group of assassins that started with one man. Solomon. He had been killed, and if it wasn't for me, he would still be alive. Solomon started the WJA when he was still the director of the FBI. He saw from the inside how this country and the so-called justice system was broken, how "we the people" didn't have the guts to fix it, and how no one on the inside wanted it fixed.

The WJA was formed with the backing of a few countries as well as some very wealthy donors here in the States. Some of them didn't know their funds were going to an underground vigilante operation, a fact that was not lost on Solomon. He created a newspaper publication called the *Global Adviser*, which was an environmental publication that circulated worldwide and claimed to be concerned about global warming, endangered bugs, and the like. I really didn't care if the earth had a fever or not; most of us regular people knew that the earth went through cycles, and it was all a part of just living on a ball out in the middle of the universe.

Sam is my daughter, and I must say, she really could beat up your honor student. I got her to take some self-defense classes, and so far, my little angel is quite the little terror on the mat. I love her more than should be allowed. She's my light, and without her, my life wouldn't be worth living.

After the incident with the Red Dog, I ended up in the infirmary at the Merc building. K stayed in my room for the first few days, and then I was sent home to recover. My head wouldn't quit hurting, and I thought the ringing in my ears was never going to go away.

I was sitting in my favorite recliner watching the news when I got the call.

"Mark," It was Kirk Weston. He was the Detroit cop whom we at the WJA somehow got to see things our way. He was *Mr. Grumpy* (he came by the nickname, honestly), but he had a good heart.

"Kirk, what is it?" I could hear something in his voice. Something I didn't like.

"Isis, she's sick. Everyone is sick… not me but, I think… I mean… You need to get down here! I'm at the hospital. Please hurry!" My mind raced, and thoughts of what it could be made my stomach turn. I wanted to tell myself that it was nothing, that this was not in any way connected to the Red Dog, but no matter how much I lied to myself, there was no way of getting around the truth.

Taras Karjanski knew something; he was so confident right before he melted into nothing. It was as if he knew something, as if he knew he had already won.

"I'm on my way."

KIRK HELD ISIS IN his arms, and he felt his heart cramp up. Isis had been standing next to him in the lobby of the Merc building talking to the receptionist when she had collapsed. "Isis!" Kirk caught her before her jet-black hair hit the marble floor, but when he looked into her eyes, he lost all hope that it was nothing serious.

Isis's Egyptian skin tones took on a pale, much lighter hue and her eyes were fluttering up in their sockets as if she was having a mini-seizure.

"Isis! Talk to me! Isis!" Kirk shook her petite frame much like a man would shake a dying comrade, hoping that he could be pulled from an awful reality. Isis did not snap out of it, and as the rest of the people in the Merc building dropped like flies, Kirk realized what was going on. Taking Isis in his arms, he pushed through the glass front doors and raced from the building.

A tall man in a business suit and a bright red tie looked as Kirk ran past, and just as he did so, the man's eyes rolled back in his head and he hit the floor with a sickening thud. Kirk did not stop and did not look back. All he knew was something in the Merc building was killing people—a virus? Was it some sort of plague, not contained to the Merc building but running wild through the streets of New York?

Looking around, he first looked up the street and stared at all the people walking and carrying on as if the world were not about to end. Isis lay limp in his arms, and Kirk could see that she was still breathing. Well, that was something, at least she was not dead. Turning uptown, Kirk ran toward the hospital. Dodging people and swearing as he knocked a woman down—Kirk ran.

"Out of my way! Move, you retarded clones, *move!*" Kirk pushed his way up the block and ran out into traffic. Horns honking and tires squealing made Kirk grimace, but he was glad the traffic was light. People were encouraged to stay indoors even after Taras Karjanski was reported dead because the President wanted to make sure the rest of the bombs had been located and all the schools in the country had undergone a complete search.

Kirk burst through the hospital doors and grabbed the first person he saw, a nurse or doctor, he didn't know and cared even less. After he shoved Isis into the pudgy man's arms, the hospital worker looked down at her lifeless body and yelled something over his shoulder. Kirk fell to the floor.

"Isis, please, no, you can't die! I love you. I need you. Not like this. Please, God, not now…" Kirk could feel hot tears well up and spill down his cheeks. He sat on the cold floor with his head buried in his hands, and he prayed. For the first time in a long time, Kirk Weston prayed.

CHAPTER TWO

MANHATTAN GENERAL WAS PURE chaos. People on stretchers lined the halls, some crying, some screaming, and some not moving at all. Doctors, nurses, and orderlies ran from one person to another, and just as I walked through the sliding doors on the west end of the hospital, a big van with "CDC" printed on the side pulled up and men in yellow hazmat suits burst from the sides and back.

"Seal off this building, I mean now—no one gets in or out!" The command was not missed by any of the people within earshot. Two guys in windbreakers bolted for the door but were stopped by the yellow-suited CDC employees.

"Let me go, man! Come on, I'm not sick, and I don't wanna get sick, man…" One of the guys was short and fat. I didn't think the man had ever jogged anywhere in his life, despite his windbreaker and jogging pants.

"Take it easy, we're not sure what we're dealing with,

and we need to test everyone so it does not spread beyond this building and the contamination site." I moved down the hall and lost site of the CDC people as I turned the corner. Kirk texted me Isis's room number. Kirk had been the first to enter the hospital, and within five minutes, the place was swarming with sick people, most of them WJA agents.

I looked around and saw many faces I recognized and some I didn't. I pushed the elevator button, and thoughts ran through my mind. Not the thoughts of a sane man, but one of a man who was dreaming.

I looked around for the signs that this was not a *glimpse*, just a dream and not the real deal. I had this gift—ability, or whatever you want to call it—I could dream of the future and see what was going to happen, but only if it had a direct impact on my life. I dreamed about Kirk once so we could find him, and that time I did control it, but I could not do that every time.

The dreams were so real that I could live a year, a month, or a week in my sleep, wake up, and have to forget the life I was living in my head. This could be a gift, but most of the time it was a curse. In a glimpse, I once lost my wife, K, and my daughter, Sam, in a bombing, and I went through a year of my life with them dead and gone. I had to move on. I met Maria and fell in love with her. K was dead, and everything that was happening was so real that I didn't know the difference.

When I woke up, K was next to me, and nothing in my dream had happened yet. But reality didn't stop the feelings I was developing for Maria. Even though I was deeply in love with K, I had this nagging feeling that I had left Maria somehow. I had spent so much time with her that my feelings were real, even though what I dreamed did not happen.

This was my curse in life. I had this other life in my head, and I had to try to find a way to control it, compartmentalize my feelings. I loved K, and I also was in love—was falling in love—with a woman I would never see again. Maria was my secretary at my old job, and now that I didn't work there anymore, there shouldn't be a problem. Shouldn't be... but even though Maria had no idea we ever had a relationship, and in her mind, she was just my secretary, in my mind and emotions, she was more than that.

The elevator opened on the fourth floor, and I made my way down the busy halls looking for room 204. Kirk would be at her side. I knew that he was falling in love with Isis. They were exact opposites, and I wondered if it would work out. Isis was a thin petite woman who was a trained assassin. She could kill without the subject ever knowing she was in the room. She was a master at stealth and one of the most effective assassins in the WJA.

Kirk was a washed-up detective from Detroit and was now sort of working with the WJA as a freelance contractor. He had some bad blood with the WJA and really wanted to find a fatal flaw so he could ruin us, or at least that was the feeling I got.

I saw Kirk walk out into the hallway. When he saw me, his face brightened. Was he happy to see me? Odd... most of the time he just put up with me, and I didn't blame him. I could be a show off at times, and he was a jerk most of the time. We had a good thing going—he left me alone, and I did the same. It seemed to work out for both of us.

"Mark, thanks for coming. Are you feeling okay?" He looked me up and down and shoved his hands in his pockets.

"Yeah, I'm fine, at least so far. What's going on?" Kirk wore a white T-shirt and a faded pair of blue jeans. His shirt used to be white but now looked a little closer to cream or a light brown because of overuse.

"Some sort of virus. The Merc building was the center…" Kirk looked into the room behind him. "She's in a bad way. Not looking good, man."

"What do you mean a virus? Like, on purpose?" I hadn't thought about this being an attack on the WJA, but now that I thought about it, I remembered what Taras had said. *"You think you can make it out of this alive?"* I thought he was talking about the sealed container he had trapped us in together. Was he talking about this virus? Had Taras done this?

"Mark, they're all dying. Everyone in the Merc building, I mean most everyone, they were all dropping like flies." I looked at him with a dazed expression on my face.

"You, what about you? You're fine."

"So far, we don't know what it is or when it will strike. We are in the middle of the hot zone now, this hospital is now the worst place to be if you're healthy."

I thought back and knew that most viruses had an incubation time. It would not just hit right away; it would take some time to grow in the host. K and Sam could have been exposed. I punched K's number on speed dial, and she answered on the third ring.

"Hey, baby, how is Isis? Is she okay?"

"I don't know yet, I just got here. Honey, it's a mess down here, I want you to stay at home and watch for any sign of illness. You and Sam may have been exposed." I tried to keep my voice calm but failed.

"What do you mean, 'exposed'? What's going on Mark?"

"We think Taras released a virus at the Merc building. Only thing is, if he did, he had to have done it when he was alive or shortly afterward, and that would mean you would have been in the building. Just stay inside, and I'll keep you updated."

"Okay, I'll check on Sam, but I feel fine. Are you—?" Her voice stopped as she asked the question. I didn't think she wanted to know the answer if it was bad news.

"I'm fine, just stay put. Don't let anyone in, and don't get the mail until I get home."

"Okay, I love you, Mark. Be careful."

"Always—love you too." I hung up, and Kirk cursed. "Let's see Isis."

KIRK SHOWED MARK INTO the room where Isis was lying hooked up to monitors and tubes. A faint beeping and a sucking sound made Kirk feel like throwing up and running from the room at the same time. Mark didn't say anything when he saw Isis, and that made him feel worse.

Kirk Weston was a man of few words, and most of the time the words he chose were negative and laced with poison. He hated to be in situations where he didn't have the upper hand, and it seemed that the WJA had him on his toes all the time. It was one thing after another—kidnapping him, holding him for a year, and (as if that wasn't enough) suckering him in to help them track down the worst terrorist ever known.

Now he was falling for one of their assassins, and he hated knowing that he couldn't control her or his feelings for her. He wished she would just blow him off so he could be done with her and the stupid agency.

He cursed under his breath again, sat down at the head of the bed, and took Isis's smooth, coffee-colored hand. Kirk felt his heart tighten and his mouth grow dry as a boil on her face marred her perfect skin. The boils had exposed themselves about five minutes ago. The doctor had given her something for the pain, and she fell asleep right before Mark showed up.

"How is she? I mean, what did the doctor say?" Mark spoke in a low voice, almost a whisper.

"They say her heart is strong, and that whatever it is…" He thought a moment, not knowing what to say beyond that. Her face and arms looked terrible, and with each passing minute, the boils grew worse. "They don't know. No one knows what it is or how to stop it. By the time they figure it out, she will be… She will be dead." He fought back stinging tears but decided it didn't matter and let them fall.

"Kirk, I'm sorry…" Mark's voice broke off, and he paced the room. Kirk felt like punching Mark. This was all his fault. If it weren't for the WJA, none of this would have happened. They provoked the Red Dog, and now they were paying for it with Isis's life.

"They say that, whatever it is, it's sucking her dry.

She is dehydrated, and even with all the fluids they are giving her, she just gets worse." Kirk tried to pull himself together. He needed to think, to try to figure this out. For Isis.

"There has to be something at Taras's condo, some sort of clue. I need to get out of here and find out what this is so I can help. Kirk, keep your phone on, and I will let you know if I find anything." Mark had a worried look on his face, but Kirk didn't know if it was because he was worried for his own family or if it was for Isis.

"Okay. Mark…?"

"Yeah?"

Kirk stood up and stepped up close so they were nose to nose. He could feel his anger rise. "You find out what this is, and you fix this! You hear? If she dies…" His voice cracked with emotion. "If she dies, I will pull this world apart to destroy you and the WJA! Do you get me?"

Mark nodded and took the warning like a man. "I won't let her die, Kirk. I swear to you, I won't let her die!"

—————

KREIOS WOKE FROM HIS dream, sat up too fast, and breathed heavily. He looked around in a panic listening for the Brotherhood. He did not hear the sounds of the woodlands or the song of birds as they made their way through the clear sky like unafraid children. His memory of his past, or maybe the past of his ancestors, brought him to the realization that he was not in the woods in his ancient land. He was sitting up in a king-size bed overlooking a long valley with a babbling brook in the bottom that wound its way through the valley and disappeared in the woods beyond.

He tossed the covers off and swung his legs to the floor. He moved with a grace that was almost inhuman. Kreios moved as if the effort of motion was not an effort at all. The bathroom light came on, and he looked at himself in the mirror.

He had thick blond hair that, in natural light, looked white. Not white of old age, but white like goose feathers. His skin was smooth and hard like granite. Muscle-bound arms and a thick neck showed that this man was not only powerful but quick as well. His skin was pale, almost transparent. Kreios splashed cool water in his face and dried it with a cream-colored towel.

The mansion was set in the side of a mountain, and the front was not visible from the road or the woods. The small tunnel that led underground would often be mistaken for an old mine shaft and was overlooked over by hikers and hunters when they came upon it.

The back of the great house, on the other hand, had a huge glass wall that looked out to the long, green valley. There was a ballroom and a large kitchen. Although the whole house had three stories with many rooms, all of them were empty. At least they were empty now.

Kreios dressed and began packing a backpack. He was going on a trip, and he would not return for quite some time. He would need some clothes and the essentials, but most of what he needed, he could buy in the city. His home was in the mountains just outside of Sun Valley, Idaho. He and a few others knew of the hidden valley, but that did not matter anymore.

Kreios threw in a set of ID cards, driver's license,

credit card, library card, and passport. He checked to make
sure that all the names matched. He used many names
but never his own. Kreios was too old a name and would
make him memorable.

Kreios finished and made his way into the kitchen for
some breakfast. He knew that he had to get the book back,
and up until now, whoever had it kept it underground
so he could not sense its presence. A few days ago, it
began calling him, and now after focusing, he was able to
pinpoint its location.

New York City.

He was not looking forward to going back to the big
city; he preferred the quiet and the solitude of his home.
But this matter would not wait, and he knew that he would
not be the only one looking for the book.

He cooked scrambled eggs, bacon, and whole-wheat
toast, and he cut a side of fruit. He took a carton of orange
juice from the huge stainless steel fridge, poured a tall
glass, and downed it in one, long gulp. Kreios ate his meal
with slow bites and sat in silence at the granite bar. He
stared out at the waterfall that cascaded over the western-
facing window. He had built this mansion over the years.
He had always wanted to live under a waterfall, and now
that he did, he couldn't think of anywhere he would rather
be. Well... that was not true. He could think of one place,
but that was another story for another time.

CHAPTER THREE

MOOCH OPENED HIS EYES and stared up at the white
ceiling tile. He had counted the tiny holes a few times over
now and wondered how long it was going to take to get
out of this hellhole. Reaching under the covers, he felt his
bare chest and touched gingerly the wrapping that covered
the place where he had been shot.

He didn't feel bad this morning, and in some ways,
he felt great. He sucked in a tentative breath, and when
no pain shot through his ribcage and no gurgling sound
escaped his lips, he smiled. This painkiller was some good
stuff. He had smoked some high-end weed and shot up a
few times, but this was even better than that. The doctors
were holding out on him, hording the good stuff under the
names of complicated drugs.

He explored the bandages with his fingers and pushed
softly, at first. When nothing happened, he pressed harder.
Hmmm… It didn't hurt, not even a little. Daring to look

down, he pushed aside the sheets and began to take off his bandages. The white gauze and wrappings were soaked in blood. The blood was somewhat dry now and made the bandages a little stiff and hard to work with.

Mooch found a spork next to his bed on the floating thingy where they put food. He used the spork to help to cut away the cloth and tape.

"This is my gift to you. All I ask is for your obedience and for full control."

The voice startled Mooch, and he looked toward the door. No one was there. He slowly scanned the room but found that he was alone. It sounded like the voice came from inside his head, as if it were his own thoughts. He remembered having a really weird dream, and, come to think of it, it was scary. He couldn't remember it all—only that something was in his room and that he was so mad at Kirk Weston.

Kirk Weston. The name brought his blood to boil instantly. He could feel a dark fog move over his brain, and he knew that, somehow, he was not alone anymore. He had been alone his whole life, but now with this… this thing in his mind, it was not altogether a bad feeling.

"We are one now. I will never leave you or forsake you." Mooch liked the way he said this. It somehow reminded him of Sunday school. His mom used to take him when he was little, before she got hooked on Meth and lost her mind. He still lived in her basement, but she was never home. He saw her three times a year, if that.

Touching his smooth skin and running his fingers over the scars, where just days before bullet holes had been— he marveled. They had completely healed. He could feel his lungs had received the same healing. Was this from God? Was this his chance to start fresh—a new life?

"This is your chance to become a real man, Mooch. You have been kicked around and beat up your whole life and now it is your turn to push back. This is your second chance to make your way, and there is one thing we must do to start this new life."

"What is that?" Mooch asked aloud.

"You know what we must do..."

Mooch did know, and just the thought of it made him smile with a lopsided grin. He remembered how Kirk left him, how he treated him, and how he hated him. "Kill Kirk Weston!"

"Yes... yes, and then you will be free!"

Mooch tossed back the sheets, found his clothes, and left the room. He walked down the hall just minutes before a van with a CDC logo on the side pulled up in front of the west entrance.

I STARTED DOWN THE east stairwell but found that the CDC had already closed it off. I couldn't waste time stuck here, and I had a feeling that whoever was in the building was not getting out for a long time. I ducked into a small room and found that it was a closet filled with lockers like some sort of break room.

I found one locker that was unlocked. Inside was a white lab coat with a nametag attached to the pocket. I pulled it on and left, heading down the elevator. I was not sure what I was going to do once I was on the ground floor.

The elevator doors opened, and I stood looking at a mass of people rushing back and forth. In the midst of the chaos, CDC employees stood at the main doors and attempted to reason with angry and scared patients.

I looked to the right toward the front sliding doors and saw that there was no way to get through. I turned left and hurried through the crowd of people. At the end of each hall, there should be an exit. I pulled the fire alarm as I passed. That really got things moving.

I spotted a yellow CDC guy standing by the door at the end of the hall, and as he looked around for the fire, I saw my chance. An older woman was arguing with him about how keeping them in here to die of smoke inhalation was murder, and I slid by the guy just as he turned to speak to the persistent woman. She yelled at him, and when she saw me go out the door, she said, "Hey, he just left! You let him leave, but we have to stay in here to die?!"

By the time the man turned and opened the door to see what the cranky woman was talking about, I was already around the corner. I spotted an ambulance with an open door as more CDC people milled around outside, doing whatever they did, about one-hundred feet from the ambulance.

I prayed the keys would be in the ignition, and my prayers were answered. With a slam of a door and a twist of the key, I was down the street and on my way downtown within minutes. Police cars were beginning to block off the streets north and south of the hospital. I turned on the lights and siren, and they waved me through—not like I was going to stop anyway.

I weaved through traffic, and as I came up to the Merc

building, I stopped in the middle of the street. Up ahead, the street was totally blocked off and the building was wrapped from top to bottom in some sort of plastic. CDC vans lined the sidewalks, police cars pulled behind the vans, and their lights flashed as traffic was diverted to the south.

I turned left and went down to the back of the building. There were not as many police or CDC vans so I figured this would be the best way in. I pulled up and slammed on the breaks so they would think I was in a hurry. I jumped out and was met by someone in a big yellow suit.

"What took you so long? And why aren't you suited up?" The man behind the yellow hazmat suit sounded annoyed, and I shrugged as if I wasn't sure what he was talking about. He pulled on my arm and ushered me to a tent with showers where others were being suited up.

"What is the status?" I asked. I wasn't sure what to say, all I knew was that I needed to get in, make sure no one found the underground center, and that all the people were up on the main level so they could get help.

The man who ushered me in helped me into a suit and showed me how to operate the respirator. "So far, no casualties, but we need all the help we can get. We found the source, but as of five minutes ago, we still have no idea what we are dealing with."

"What started all this?" I pulled on the hood and the tall man answered.

"A dead dog sprayed with some sort of airborne toxin. We're not sure if it's a virus or if it is just a toxin. Either way, it seems to be contained to the building and Manhattan General. Some idiot brought a girl in, so now we have to contain two sites."

I nodded and followed him in through a maze of plastic tunnels and two sets of different air locks and showers. When we finally made it into the building, the tall man patted me on the back and stayed at the entrance. I walked through the sliding doors and into a hallway that led to the elevators and beyond the lobby.

I was expecting the place to be much like the hospital, but to my surprise, it was mostly deserted. I nodded to the suited up guard and walked on down the hall and into the main lobby. White cots were lined up, over a hundred people were lying, end to end, on the cots, and the sight made me shudder.

I looked again for anyone I might know but didn't see anyone… I was worried for Big B and some of the others. I looked out over the scene and noticed that there were only five doctors in hazmat suits. *How come so few are helping with so many sick?*

Okay, Mark, let's get going, there is nothing you can do here. The best way you can help is to find out who brought this dead dog in and run the surveillance tapes for… then something hit me. I was not sick, Kirk was not sick, and so far, K and Sam were not sick. There had to be a time when all of us who were not infected were out of the building at the same time. Or maybe, just maybe, we had some sort of immunity to whatever this virus was.

I turned to the row of elevators. When they opened, I walked in, punched in the correct sequence, and the elevator dropped. The elevator was one of a kind. It was built so that it could not only travel up and down, but side to side as well. The WJA headquarters was under the

Merc building. The only way down was by using a code, and even then, that would only get you as far as the front lobby.

When the doors opened, I was overcome with the silence of the place. Usually, the activity was bustling, and the lobby had the draw of adventure to it, but this was like a graveyard. I went through security and took off my suit. It was hard to move and look around with eighteen pounds of plastic strapped to your body.

It took me an hour to go through the underground center. I didn't find anyone. I was glad, but at the same time, it scared me. I was not used to being alone in the WJA center. After concluding my search, I made my way to the control room.

The control room was where all the security cameras were linked in. They oversaw the Merc building as well as other outside locations of interest. I sat down in front of the five hundred monitors and began searching for anything that might help. We knew what the object was that triggered the virus, and we knew some of us were either not exposed or immune. But why?

I found the footage of the handsome black UPS man as he brought in the package. I followed him up to its final destination and even saw the poor secretary who opened it. The dead, rotting dog made her scream, and she almost fell over because she was so scared. I marked the day, time of the delivery, and began going through the footage.

I pulled up the infirmary and saw that at the exact time of the delivery, I was in bed sleeping, and K and Sam were sitting close by playing Go Fish. So much for being immune.

Isis woke up. Kirk stood up quickly and hovered over her like a scared rabbit. "Are you okay? How are you feeling?" He was panting hard, and his face was lined with worry. Isis licked her lips and tried to speak, but all that came out was a dry croak.

Kirk handed her a plastic cup of water with a bendy straw. She took it and drank all the liquid. She sighed, looked at her arm where the IV was inserted and shook her head. She had a few more boils, and her once smooth skin was now blotchy and covered with open sores. "I'm fine… I mean…" Her voice cracked, and she smiled weakly at Kirk. "I guess I'm not fine, am I?"

Kirk kissed her hand and wiped her forehead with a cool cloth. "They're doing everything they can, but no one around here seems to know what it is or what to do to stop it!" He was so frustrated, and seeing Isis like this was killing him.

Isis nodded toward the empty cup, and Kirk refilled it from the sink in the bathroom. She drained the second glass, closed her eyes, breathed in deep, and let it out slowly. "Where is Mark? Is he okay?" Kirk ground his teeth and swore under his breath. *How could she be worried about Mark at a time like this? Doesn't she know…?* Then he remembered that she was the first to get sick, so she might not know that she wasn't the only one.

"Isis, this is more than just some random thing. The entire Merc building is locked down, and the CDC has also locked this hospital down. They say it's some sort of outbreak." Isis looked at Kirk with wide eyes and tried to sit up. She was pushed gently back down by Kirk's strong hand.

"What? What are you talking about?"

"Isis, this was an attack on us, er… you guys. Mark thinks he knows who it was. He thinks it was Taras. He and I are the only ones that seem to not be affected by the virus, but that may be just a false hope. I could still get sick. Maybe it's just taking longer with us." Kirk tried to hide his anger toward Mark, but wasn't doing a very good job.

"Kirk, if you can get whatever I have, you need to leave. Stay away from me. I don't want you to get sick." Kirk laughed and shook his head.

"Too late, we're stuck now, they won't let anyone out until they figure out what this is and how to stop it—or until we all die." Isis frowned and coughed hard. Kirk helped her to a sitting position, and he looked into her dark, almost black, eyes. Her eyes were so beautiful, so knowing, as if she could look into his very soul.

"Don't look at me like that, Kirk Weston. You are going to make me cry, and I do not cry, mister." Isis touched his face, and Kirk leaned down and kissed her on the forehead.

"You will be fine, kiddo. Mark is going to find out what is going on, and he promised to find the cure. All you have to do is hang in there." Kirk knew that, even though Mark promised to fix this, it was not something he had the right to promise. No one could control this, and he of all people was beginning to understand how little control he had over his own destiny.

Kirk and Isis talked for a few more minutes before a

doctor came back in to take some blood. He wore a type of mask and asked to take Kirk's blood as well. "You are not sick yet, and we need to see if we can track this virus as it moves along."

The doctor was a short man with a thick crop of black hair. He had good bedside manner, so Kirk didn't object. After he drew his blood, Kirk asked. "So tell me, Doc, what are we looking at here? How bad is it?"

The doctor shook his head and said. "It isn't looking good. We have a few patients over at the Merc building who have already died. It is moving fast, and we still don't know how to effectively treat it. All we can do is treat the symptoms, and try to keep the patients as comfortable as possible." Kirk looked back to Isis, who had fallen asleep again. Her face was scrunched up as if she were in pain or having a bad dream or something.

You better hurry up, Mark. You better not have lied to me… You promised… you promised!

CHAPTER FOUR

"LADIES AND GENTLEMEN, THE president of the
United States of America." The announcer ended his
introduction and left the stage where a blue curtain hung
behind a podium with the presidential seal. The president
moved to the center of the stage as flashes filled the air
and the sounds of clicking and whispers floated through
the room.

Standing tall and adjusting his navy blue tie, the
president began. He was not sure how to feel about
the state of the country under his leadership, and even
though he knew that the terrorist attacks were not his fault
directly, he took full responsibility for the fear the country
was experiencing, and he was saddened to have to prolong
his people's anxiety.

Most of his speeches were written for him, and all
were filled with calming words and in turn did not say
much. He knew this could backfire, but he decided to

speak from his heart despite his aide's disapproving glares.

"Tonight, I stand before you with a victory as well as a problem. I, like a father, look out over this country and think of you as my own children. I want to talk to you as a family, as I hope that you, the American people, feel the same way. This is no longer about politics or the side of the aisle on which you find yourselves; we are at a time in our country's history that will define the landscape of our future and the future of our children and our grandchildren." He took a sip from a glass of water and wiped sweat from his brow. He believed in the saying, "Never let them see you sweat," so he felt like running from the stage and hiding under his desk.

"The terrorist known as the Red Dog has been killed, his comrades have been detained, and more are being pursued. Taras Karjanski was killed resisting arrest and will no longer be roaming our streets and killing at will. Let it be known: we will not be put under the thumb of fear or hate. Today, we stand strong. Today, we stand as one, and today, we have won!"

The crowd of reporters and representatives roared with applause and hooted in agreement. The president smiled, but hidden in his heart was the fact that he had to depend on some vigilante group to do what the FBI and CIA should have done. He ran his hand through his salt-streaked hair and waited for the crowd to settle down.

"We have won this battle, but the war is far from over. We still have to deal with the oil refineries that have been destroyed and the fallout that will come from lack of oil. I ask you, the American people, to take thought of tomorrow and work with each other so we can get through this period as quickly as possible. Now more than ever, we see the need to quit talking about alternative fuel and do something about it. Now more than ever, we need to cut off our dependence on foreign oil and be self-dependent.

"I have commissioned the US oil taskforce to begin drilling right here in America. However, this process will take time, and in the meantime, we still have to drive and carry on with our lives. There will be a restriction on fuel for individuals and businesses in effect immediately. Each person of driving age will be given credits every month. Businesses will be given credits to use for fuel. These credits will depend on the use of transportation, and if you do not have to travel, we urge you to stay close to home or find other ways to get from one place to another." Questions flew up as he paused, but he held up his hand, and everyone quieted.

"More information will come out in the days to come. We all know that this will be a major setback, but what I do not want is oil prices to keep climbing. We are in the process of working with our neighboring countries in order to enact this credit system worldwide. This situation affects all of us, and now that we know where these attacks came from, we must work together and put policies in place to keep this from ever happening again. We are on the dawn of a new world, and one in which we can no longer afford to fight amongst ourselves. Now is the time to stand together. Now is the time to unite!"

The room trumpeted with cheers and clapping. Reporters yelled out questions and the president held up his hand, palm out. After the crowd calmed, the president continued. "The other matter we need to address is the virus that has broken out in New York City. The source is unknown, but the effect is contained at this time. Manhattan General and the Merc building are the two locations where the virus has been detected, and these buildings have been quarantined. The effects of this virus are not spreading to others, and it is believed that only the directly exposed are in any danger. I ask you to please keep calm and let the CDC take care of this matter. They are trained and will find a cure for this virus. Our main concern is to keep this from spreading and to help the people who have been exposed to this virus."

"Is this virus another terrorist attack?" A reporter from USA Today managed to get a question in. The president looked at him and decided to answer.

"We have confirmation that this was the last act of the terrorist known as Taras Karjanski. He sent the virus in the mail and chose the Merc building as his main target. We will release more information as it is available. The main thing is to stay calm and let the CDC do its job."

Taking another sip of water, the president looked out over the silent crowd. He marveled at how a group of reporters could be so quiet, but in times like this, the news gave way to humanity. They were all in this together, and even if it would be brief, they felt it too.

"I have one more matter to discuss concerning Taras Karjanski. He threatened our children and did indeed blow up a school. I will not allow this to happen again on my watch. The authorities are in the process of going through every school in this country to search for any explosives. Until this process is complete, school will be postponed until further notice. Every family with students in school from the grade of twelve on down will have the option to keep up online. Classes will be streamed live, via the internet. A website has been set up, so all you have to do is register your child, follow the simple steps, and continue their education in this manner until we deem it safe to return to normal classes."

The press conference went on for over two more hours, with the director of the FBI, the secretary of education, and the energy commissioner speaking after the president. The president felt that they were now on the right track. He needed to stop the bleeding before the country died. He knew that fear and panic would follow, but he prayed it would be small and scattered.

I CALLED K AGAIN and was relieved to find that she was still okay with no sign of an outbreak. "And Sam?"

"Sam is fine. I'm worried about you. They say that the virus is not spreading, that's good right?" I was out of the loop and hadn't made it to a TV in some time, so K filled me in on what the president said in his address. I was glad they pulled back the military and retracted martial law. The people needed to feel safe and nothing said you are not safe like tanks and soldiers with guns walking down every street and standing on the corner in front of Walmart.

"So did he say what this virus is?" I didn't think he would know anything more than we did here on the ground, but it was worth a shot.

"No, just that it isn't spreading. How is Isis?"

I shuddered at the thought of her lying so helpless and weak. She was such a strong woman, and to see her like that unnerved me. I had to find out what we were dealing with and why I wasn't sick.

"She's fine for now, but it's getting worse by the minute. I think she'll die soon if something isn't done. Can you think of any reason you, me, and Sam wouldn't get it?"

"What about Kirk? He's fine, too, right?"

"Yeah, it seems like it is random: some are getting sick and some aren't. I wonder what the trigger is."

"Have you tried to dream?" The question caught me off guard.

"No, I don't think it works that way. I can't just pull up a menu and pick what I want to see. I can dream of the future but I don't think the past."

"Well have you ever tried? If it doesn't work, you are no worse off."

I figured she was right. I was not one to quit, and if I even had a tiny chance of glimpsing into the past, I wanted to try. "I've never even tried. But you are right, I have nothing now, and if it might help, I'll give it a shot." I decided that Solomon's old office would work the best. It was deep underground, and no one would disturb me there. I hung up with K and promised to call her after I was done to let her know how it went.

I took the elevator as it moved deeper underground and then began to move sideways through a long dark tunnel. The sides of the elevator were made of glass, so I could see through on all sides. No matter how many times I walked around down here and saw everything the WJA could do, it still amazed me.

The double doors opened, and the main lobby with a tall desk where Solomon's secretary used to sit was empty. I pushed the large, heavy, wooden door to his office open, and the smell of leather and paper filled my lungs. He had thousands of books lining the walls in oak bookshelves. The dim lighting gave the office a mysterious feel, and I could still smell the scent of pipe smoke.

There was a large leather sofa, and I fumbled in my pocket for some sleeping pills. I did not have a hard time sleeping, but when I needed to dream (or glimpse, as I called it) sometimes I needed some help. I popped two in my mouth and chewed them. The taste didn't bother me. After using it so many times, I got used to it.

I lay down, and my head spun with all the things I had to do. I thought about Kirk and the expression on his face as he looked at Isis. He was so distraught and filled with grief of the unknown. I tried to clear my mind and to think about Taras. I hated him, and even though he was dead, I didn't want to think about him or see through his eyes again.

I did it once before and I had no desire to do it again, but I didn't have a better plan, so I focused. I let the package with the dead dog in it fill my mind. I tried to replay every detail of what it looked like, the color of the brown cardboard, the shipping label, and the way the UPS guy carried it under his arm.

I brought up Taras in my mind, thought of his features, and willed myself to see him. The scar above his eye, and the way his hair hung in black and silver around his ears. His sneer and the smell of Vodka on his breath. He was so dark and evil. I remembered the way his mind felt as I saw from his eyes. The way it wrapped around me like a warm blanket, but tight as a vice. I didn't want to go there, but I had to go.

Kirk and Isis were depending on me, the WJA was depending on me, and I was the only one who could save them. I had one shot at this, and if it failed, I was out of ideas. My eyes grew heavy and my arms and legs fell limp as I began to drift off into whatever world I went to in glimpses.

I never thought about it before, but what made me so different that I could dream of the future, or of the past, for that matter? How did I escape the grave and kill Taras only days ago? Where did that light that freed me come from, and how could I explain that I killed a man with no weapon but with some sort of light that shot from my body?

I wondered if it was stress or some sort of reflex that kicked in so I would stay alive. I didn't have the answer, and as I fell into a glimpse, my last thought was why... not of Taras, not of Kirk, or of Isis, but just the question. *Why?*

CHAPTER FIVE

KREIOS BOARDED THE 747 and didn't mind thinking how stupid it was to fly like this. He hated the smell of recycled air and the feel of the pop can these people called advanced technology. He found his seat in first class and sat down heavily, breathing in a sigh of relief. No, it was anxiety, and now not only would this flight take too much time, but the pull of the book was stronger. It was in danger; he could feel it.

After ten minutes, all the other passengers were seated, and the door was sealed shut. He didn't like closed-in spaces, and he could feel sweat bead up on his forehead as the slim stewardess asked him if he wanted something to drink.

"I would love some water, if you don't mind." He glanced at the blonde with a look she did not get often. He was not in the least interested in her, not even a little hint of desire behind his eyes, which made her try even harder.

Kreios was an old man, but he did not appear a day over thirty-five.

"Right away, sir. Where are you going, if you don't mind my asking?" She batted her lashes and bent down a little too far as she reached for a bottle of spring water. She was wearing a white button up top, the standard for this airline, and a black, knee-length skirt. She chose to wear a size too small, and Kreios knew from her looks and the way she carried herself that she was used to being flirted with.

"New York. I have some property I have to pick up from a friend." Kreios could see if he did not play the part, this woman would hound him the entire trip asking questions, and the last thing he wanted was to have to answer any more questions.

"I see you have no wedding ring. Are you a single woman, or am I barking up the wrong tree?" He touched her arm and looked into her eyes with the skill of many years of studying the art of seduction.

"I am. I have a boyfriend, though, back home in Quincy." Her answer was not convincing and he could see she was a little disappointed that the game was not going as she hoped.

"Well, I was asking because I have this friend, he is such a good guy, a little misguided and not much into… well you know how it is, these men nowadays love to play video games, and real people are not really in their reality."

Her eyes grew dark, and the smile faded into the fake one she reserved for people that she didn't really want to know or talk to. Kreios smiled and pulled out a pen. "Do you mind if I give him your number?" He wanted to laugh and put her out of her misery, but he knew this was the only way to keep her from pestering him.

"I, uh… Well I don't think that would be a good idea. I do have a boyfriend, so I think he might be mad if I gave out my number to just any stranger. You understand? More water?" She offered him the bottle, and he took it with a disappointed frown.

"Oh, I am sorry. I thought it would be a good match, you are so pretty and all. Sorry for the misunderstanding." Kreios took the bottle and the blonde moved on muttering to herself. Kreios took a sip, lay back in his seat, and closed his eyes. He thought about the book and hoped he would not have any trouble with Kirk and Mark. He was looking forward to meeting both men, especially Mark Appleton.

⌘

MOOCH MOVED DOWN THE back alley in between the hospital and the tall, brick building next door. He found a jacket on his way out and took it to cover up his ugly baby-blue hospital gown. He was barefoot and hungry—man, was he hungry.

Looking around as he came to the street, he hailed a cab and got in. The cabbie was a scruffy man much like Mooch, in a way. Skinny and covered with hair on his face, neck and all over his head like tangles of soft wire. Mooch told him the address of his house, and the driver started the meter.

How are you going to pay for the cab ride?

Mooch could hear his own thoughts, but he knew that

these thoughts were not his own but of the thing that was inside of him. He didn't mind, in fact, it made him feel good. More than good—great. As if he was powerful, as if he was in costume and could do anything.

As he pondered his dilemma, a brilliant idea struck him. "Driver, can you pull around the block? I can get out here if that works for you." The cab driver nodded and pulled into a deserted alley. Mooch could see it all in his mind— the way the alley was hidden from the street, and the way it was dark and closed in on the end. Like in a movie he once saw, he reached for the thin drawstring that was looped around his waist. It was supposed to help to keep the back of his gown closed, but it failed the job in every way.

Pulling it free he wound each end around his wrists, and in seconds, had it around the driver's neck. He yanked back, braced his feet on the back of the seat, and used all his body weight to strangle the cabbie.

The driver gagged and clawed at the noose around his neck as he hit the gas. The cab lurched forward and began to gain speed. Mooch pulled tighter, and he could see the driver's face in the rearview mirror. What a sight, he was so red, and his face was wrenching like nothing he had ever seen. *Good, keep it tight. Now brace yourself!*

Looking up, Mooch saw a brick wall looming ahead and a moment later, the cab plowed into the wall at thirty miles per hour. The force drove the cab driver forward, and as Mooch pulled back on the makeshift noose, the cab drivers windpipe collapsed and he was dead before the last piece of glass fell to the pavement.

Mooch was breathing hard, and after a full minute,

he released his hold on the drawstring. He got out, walked around to the driver's side, and opened the door. Somehow, the front of the car didn't have much damage. The cabbie had a bright red line across his throat, and his eyes bulged in horror. Mooch pulled the man from his seat, got in, and backed up. He needed a ride, and this cab would be just the ticket. He looked similar to the cabbie, and nothing blended in better than a yellow cab in New York City.

Mooch pulled out of the alley, merged with the slow moving traffic, and headed for his house, well not his house, but his good-for-nothing Mom's house. He looked at his hands and noticed that they were shaking. He had never killed anyone before, and the feeling was… it was— wonderful, the best feeling ever. Having the power to end a life was something only God should have the power to do, and now he felt like he understood God a little more because of his connection with him. He, just like God, decided to kill, and now he was not just another nobody. He was somebody.

"I am coming for you, little Kirky. I am going to kill you and show you what it is like to suffer, to be the butt of all the jokes." Mooch drove on and knew that this was the start to a new life—a better life.

THE SKY WAS DARK. Thick, low-hanging clouds covered the moon, and a chill saturated the air. I could feel pure evil run through my mind as I looked out through the eyes of the worst madman this world had seen in a long time. He was dead, but here in my dreams, he lived, and the thought gave me the creeps. Could he somehow come back through me or maybe cross over to this life through this weird experience? I didn't know, but the idea still made me shiver.

I was in his penthouse, sometime before his doom. He, or rather I, looked around as I became him. I looked down at my watch and at the date. It was a month before the encounter in which he died, and I changed forever.

The phone rang in my pocket, so I picked it up and answered. "Hello?" My voice sounded strange in my ears and I was speaking Russian. I never learned Russian nor did I understand the language, yet here I was, speaking it and understanding just fine. This glimpse stuff had some cool things going on. I made a mental note to think about this further, and maybe do some more research.

"We have the virus formulated and the antidote ready. We are prepared to show you a demonstration, sir, whenever you are ready." The voice on the other end was from an older man, and by his tone I could tell that he was scared.

"I will come by this afternoon. This better be right, or I will not show your family any more mercy." I was not the one talking, but I was somehow along for the ride. It was a weird sensation.

Taras shut the phone and took the elevator down to a parking garage. Waiting for him was a black Mercedes with a driver who didn't say one word, but just opened the door for his boss and pulled the car out onto the overcrowded streets. After an hour, the car pulled in an underground garage and parked. Taras got out and walked to an elevator. From the looks of the building and the number of floors, I figured this was some sort of industrial complex.

Five floors and we ended up on the second. A man in his late fifties wearing a white lab coat met Taras. His hands shook as he spoke. "Welcome back, sir," His Russian was good. He was from the old country—I don't know how I knew this, but I did.

"Show me the virus." Taras's mind raced with images of what he wanted to do to this doctor, and it made me want to gag. I wished I could close my eyes or turn off this sick freak's mind. How could a person get to this point? He was so filled with hate and violence.

The man... what was his name? I searched Taras's memory but came up empty.

Taras followed the man in the lab coat through a set of steel double doors and into a wide-open room. The place was clean and housed tables and equipment. Test tubes, burners, and other such devices covered all the open counter space. Two other men worked with their heads down, and I could feel their fear as well.

"The human trial worked better than we expected, the subject is in his first week of exposure and is showing signs of extreme decomposition." Taras looked through a window on the far end of the room into a small white cube that revealed one bed with a man strapped in and hooked up to tubes and machines.

My heart sank.

"What are his symptoms?" Taras was all business and from his thought pattern, he had no feelings toward the man they had kidnapped for this trial. "When will he die?"

"Fever, rashes, boils, elevated heart rate, labored

breathing—"

"When will he die?"

The lab coat shook his head and said. "Three days, maybe four." He looked at the ground and shifted his feet. "I was hoping to use the antidote and see if we could save him."

"No, we wait until he is knocking on death's door… and even then I will have to see." Taras did not intend to give the antidote to anyone. It was his way of giving the man a false hope. Taras wanted to give the impression that he was trying to save people, not unleash a virus on his own people. All he wanted the antidote for was himself.

"But—"

"But? How much do you have? I told you to only make enough for one person. All we need to do is know that we have the capabilities to manufacture an antidote, and set the price. The government will pay us anything to mass produce the stuff once I…" Taras slipped… the great Taras slipped, and the look on the lab coat's face showed a mix of fear and anger.

The lab coat lowered his eyes and said in a tense voice. "This is not for you to use as your little play thing, this is so we can create an antidote for what may come. I have no intention of letting you kill anyone else with this… this virus!"

The heat in my head boiled, and I saw my hand come up so fast that I didn't have time to even think of what was happening. The gun in my hand jerked, and the face of the old man had that look of shock and deadness all at the same time.

A small circle of blood formed on his forehead and his

knees buckled. The back of his head was gone, and as he hit the floor, the two other men stood up from their chairs and scrambled like drowning rats.

"No!" I screamed in his head, all the time knowing that I was a passenger and had no control. Taras was dead and this was just a memory I had somehow entered into.

"Stop!" The command worked on one of the men, but the other one ran for the door. A red spot formed on the man's back, and he fell as Taras squeezed the trigger and sent a .22 caliber bullet through his spine. It was a great shot, the guy had to be fifty feet from where Taras stood, and he was running. I chided myself for taking note of the shot, but I was, after all, a killer myself.

"If you value your life, you will not move." The man who stood frozen with his hands up in the air in the surrender position turned to face Taras.

"Please don't shoot, I have a family…"

"What makes you think I care if you have a family? Where is the virus, how much do you have?" The man wiped a hand across his brow, and his thick, black hair clung to his skull laced with sweat.

"Over here, in the storage room, it has to be incubated below zero. We have a special freezer set up to keep it cold."

"What happens if it thaws out?" Taras asked.

The man looked around and, as if unsure of himself, said. "It becomes airborne and will activate. Once active, it will become transferable in four to six hours."

"Transferable?" Taras moved closer and stopped just a few feet from where the trembling man stood. He smiled as he smelled the urine in the air.

"Lethal. It will pass from one host to another, and anyone in the area of impact will become infected. It has a short shelf life once airborne, but it can spread fast."

"And the antidote?"

"We have just one injection, just like you wanted." The man relaxed a little, and Taras nodded.

"Good, please show me the storage room."

"Yes, sir, right this way." Taras took a few steps and looked down at the man who lay face down in a growing pool of blood. His heart jumped a beat, and I could sense that this site made him happy… almost euphoric.

The dark-haired man entered a combination to the freezer door and opened the five-by-five box. Inside were three vials with a clear liquid in them. "And where is the antidote?"

"Over here," He pointed to a small glass case, and inside was a syringe filled with a red liquid on one end and a dark black liquid on the other end. "The two will mix as you inject the subject. It should work in less than an hour—I mean it will work..." The man stuttered, and the sound of a gunshot relieved him of any future stuttering problems. Taras watched him as he fell to the floor. He put two more rounds in his head just for the fun of it.

"Thank you for your service." He grunted and returned his weapon to its holster just inside his coat. He placed two of the vials in the cooler and shut the lid. He grabbed the last vial, tossed it across the room, and smiled as it shattered against the far wall.

I needed to find out what he did with the antidote. I could feel the dream slipping, but I held on, forcing myself to stay under just for a moment longer. The sound of a clock ticked, and I could now feel a faint breathing motion as I slept. Then all at once, the glimpse vanished, and I was awake.

CHAPTER SIX

KIRK STOOD ON THE brink of madness. He hated to
be tied down, and this situation was making him go stir
crazy. The hospital was sealed up tight, and Isis seemed
to be stable, but she wasn't getting better. Kirk paced the
hallway and walked up and down the stairs as he thought
through his options.

He hated Mark and his involvement with the WJA, and
he hated even more the man who was responsible for Isis's
condition. *You better pull through, Mark.* He didn't want
to think about it, and sitting here made him feel worthless.

Isis was asleep when he stuck his head in her room
and sighed. "I know I've no right to be talking to you
or anything," Kirk looked up and his eyes burned with
tears. He couldn't remember the last time he prayed,
really prayed, but he couldn't think of anything else to do.
"Please, God, I know you have the power to take or give
life. I love her so much I can't even tell you. Good things

don't come my way that often, and I beg you, please help her..." He paused and said, "Thanks."

Kirk wiped his eyes with the back of his hand, turned, and walked down to the elevators. He made his way to the cafeteria and bought a coffee and a bagel. His cell phone vibrated in his pocket; he had turned down the ringer because he was not supposed to use it in the hospital.

"Hello."

"Kirk—Mark. I found something." Mark sounded exhausted.

"Did you find the antidote? Tell me what you found!" Kirk's hands trembled, and he had the phone pushed up to his ear hard so as not to miss one word.

"Calm down, I am doing the best I can. Remember that I have known Isis longer then you and care deeply for her. We're on the same side." Mark's voice was strained, and Kirk took a deep breath.

"Sorry, it's just that I... what did you find out?" He wanted to say he loved her but couldn't get the words past his lips, not to anyone but him and her... and maybe God.

"I got in his head, it was creepy."

"What do you mean, 'his head'?"

"I dreamed... I concentrated and got into a memory inside of Taras's head."

"How is that possible?"

"I don't know... I know he is dead, but somehow I was able to see into the past..."

"Okay, so what happened?" Kirk didn't know if he believed it, but he would take anything right now.

"Taras created the virus by blackmailing some physicists, and he ended up with two vials. One at the

WJA building and the other one... I don't know. He made one injection of the antidote for himself, and then he killed everyone... it was horrible."

"Where is the antidote?" Kirk held his breath.

"I don't know, I lost the glimpse... but he took it with him, so it has to be somewhere in his penthouse or maybe in—"

"—the penthouse? The place is a bombsite. Whatever was there is long gone! You have to go back in his head... you have to find it." Kirk spilled his coffee as he stood up. The dark liquid ran across the table and dripped onto the cold, tile floor.

"I know, Kirk, but it doesn't work like that. I can't just go in and pick a spot. This was a one-time thing, I don't even know how I did it."

"We have to do something, she's dying! Do you understand that?" Kirk could feel the anger begin to rise to the surface, and the sting of more tears crept into his eyes and voice.

"I know... I am going over to his place, and I will search everything that is there. Maybe on another floor... or in a safe—safes are fireproof."

"I'm coming with you."

"You can't, you're trapped in that hospital. Besides, you need to stay with Isis." Kirk hung up the phone and sat down. He had to think, had to find a way out of this place. He couldn't just sit here and do nothing. He had to do something.

A BRIGHT LCD SCREEN glowed in the dark room

as Mooch took in the feeling of the color and light as it caressed his face. It was just him and his computers, and of course, a box of hot pizza—pepperoni and black olives.

He had four monitors set up in a semicircle and one master keypad, one of the new ones that could roll up and looked more like a thin plastic placemat than a keyboard. Mooch stopped by one of his favorite computer geek places and took what he wanted. The shop was closed, so no one had to die. He found the secret room that he knew existed from the many times he had been in the business in the past. He always wanted to go down there and check it out, but the storeowner wouldn't let anyone in that room.

Mooch saw why, the place was full of black-market parts, and most of the stuff wasn't even on the market yet. Mooch figured he had a connection with a manufacturer and was testing products for them, or he had a much darker connection.

The screen changed, and without much effort he was in Kirk Weston's bank account. He drained it and put an alert on all his credit cards. "There goes your one million dollars!" Well, not one million now, more like $856,300.98, living in Bali and the villa took a chunk out of his original amount.

Next, he broke into the FBI website and made Kirk Weston of the Detroit Police Department come back from the dead. He was enjoying the life of a dead man, after all the world believed him to have died in an explosion over a year ago. Not only was he alive now, but he was wanted for murder, even made the top 100 list for America's Most Wanted. "Congrats, pal... you murderer you."

Mooch smiled, and he took a big bite from a slice of pizza. He typed with the other hand, and his fingers moved with skillful speed. "Shall we put your face out there, my old friend?"

After Mooch was done with phase one, Kirk Weston's face was on the six o'clock news, and it went something like this.

"Kirk Weston was assumed dead after he was kidnapped over a year ago but turned up alive just last week. Surveillance footage shows him leaving the scene of a crime in West Hollywood where he is suspected of murdering a family as they slept. This Ex-Detroit detective has a record of violence and abuse. He was suspended upon further investigation into a rape charge when he disappeared last year. Kirk Weston is armed and dangerous, if you have any information leading to the arrest and conviction, please call the hotline on your screen."

Mooch not only tied him to a open case, but created a tape and tied him in with DNA evidence all somehow ending up in the file and evidence log at the West Hollywood police CSI office. The detective in charge couldn't remember logging any of this in, and got a butt chewing from the captain for missing important information.

All it took was some creative video editing, a few well placed emails to the local news stations, and last of all some record changes in the FBI database. Kirk Weston now had a past and a not-so-bright future. He would be running from the Feds, the cops, and him. Only thing was, he didn't even know that Mooch was after him… which made it so much more fun.

I HUNG UP THE phone and shook my head. Kirk was so stubborn, I knew he was going to try to break out of the hospital and go to the bombed out penthouse across from the Merc building. I left Solomon's office and took the elevator up to the main level. I needed to suit up and at least be prepared for whatever I might run into.

I was the only one in the lower levels of the building, and as I pulled on the second skin, I felt something, or someone, watching me. I looked around and saw nothing. I was in a small room with glass cases surrounding the room, and hanging in all of them were the suits we called "second skin." These suits would mold to the host body and could keep your body cool. It was also bulletproof. It was light and thin and could be worn under regular clothes.

I pulled on a pair of blue jeans and a black t-shirt. My blond hair was spiked up, and as I tied the laces to my boots, I looked up and felt that same feeling that I was being watched. "Hello?" I sounded stupid calling out in an empty building, but I couldn't shake the feeling.

The sounds of machines running and the quiet beeping and clicking of computers hummed in the background, but other than that, all was quiet.

I left the room and turned to go down the hall, and all my senses went off at one time. The hair on the back of my neck stood on end, and I could feel my heart race and then slow as my instincts kicked in. I had a knife in my hand, and I crouched, alert and ready. Standing at the far end of the hall was a man with a backpack slung over his shoulder. He was tall and powerful. Just the way he stood commanded respect.

I looked at him, and he stared at me with an amused expression on his face. He had smooth, white skin, almost translucent, and markings from some sort of tattoo or birthmark crawled up his neck. "Who are you?" I asked.

He didn't move and just stood, feet planted, as if to keep me from getting past him. When he spoke, I could feel it in my head and ears as if he were speaking right into my brain. It was a weird sensation—unnerving. "Mark, I have been waiting a long time to meet you. My name is Kreios. I was wondering if I may have a word with you."

My hand gripped the knife at my hip, and as he shifted his feet, all my instincts screamed danger. I rushed forward, but before I could take one step, he closed the distance and took hold of my throat faster than anyone should be able to move. "I am not here to hurt you, but I will if necessary." His voice was calm and hard. I struggled to breathe as his hand cut off my air supply.

I looked down to my other hand and at the blade that was buried up to the hilt in the side of his neck. I smiled and watched as a line of red blood oozed from the wound. "I pull this knife," I croaked, "and you die!"

It was his turn to smile. It was a weird smile, as if it was foreign to his face, and I got the feeling that this man didn't smile all that much. He released his grip on my throat and stepped back. I let go of the knife and gasped for air. He took hold of the knife handle and pulled it from his neck, and I held out my left hand to stop him. He would die if he released the plug and tore the artery open.

"No... don't!" I hissed.

He flipped the knife over and handed it back to me, handle first. I stared up at him, noticing for the first time how tall he was. He had to be almost seven feet tall, and his arms were thick and defined. I could see muscle ripple as he moved, and a part of me stood in awe.

"I will be fine, I was hoping to bring you into this at a slower pace, but I see you are a man of action." Kreios took his hand from the cut on his neck and I watched in shock as the wound closed up and sealed over with fresh skin. In seconds, the gash was gone; he wiped the blood from his neck and wiped his hands on his pants.

"Who are you?" I stood up and my mind raced. This was not possible, but then again, the things I could do were not possible.

"Let us talk over a cup of coffee. You do drink coffee, do you not?"

I nodded, and the questions that flooded my mind didn't let up. I followed him from the building, past the CDC workers, and we walked down a block to the small café I liked to visit with K. How did he know me, who was he, and how did he get into the building? He just walked in as if he owned the place.

"Relax, the answers will come."

Did he just read my mind?

CHAPTER SEVEN

STIR CRAZY WAS A mild term to describe Kirk. He
paced Isis's room and looked at her as she slept. He could
only think of her dying as he sat around doing absolutely
nothing, like a lame side character in some boring, subpar
movie.

He muttered a curse, opened the door, and looked out
into the hall where CDC goons milled about in their bright
yellow suits and doctors rushed in and out of rooms with
drawn looks on their faces. The place had the smell of
death, and Kirk couldn't help feeling trapped and alone.
He didn't like the feel, the smell, or the hopelessness so
apparent in everyone's eyes.

Moving to Isis's side, he touched her smooth cheek
with his hand. Her eyes fluttered open, he looked into their
deep pools of darkness, and his heart quivered in his chest.

"Hey, kiddo, how you doing?"

Isis forced a smile and breathed in deep as if to gain

some strength to answer.

"Great." Her voice was harsh and strained. Kirk took her hand and kissed each finger, and she smiled at him.

"You look like death. You should do your hair or something." Kirk managed a lopsided grin, and Isis squeezed his hand. "Look, I'm getting out of here. Mark thinks he knows where the antidote is, and I have to help him. I can't just sit here and watch you—" His voice cut off, and he looked down at the floor.

"No... stay. Please?" Isis pleaded. She was so weak that it made the plea even more powerful. Kirk shook his head.

"I have to save you; I am not going to sit around. You know I have to go... Isis, you know how I feel about you. I can't lose you..." Kirk could feel the sting of tears welling up in his eyes, and he fought them back. Standing up, he turned and left the room, not daring to look back, knowing that if he did he would never leave.

With a soft thud, the door shut. His eyes burned, and he allowed a stream to flow down and wiped them away with the back of his hand. This was not the time to cry. She was alive, but not if he kept standing here like a lovesick idiot.

Turning, he walked down the hall toward the elevators, not sure what he was going to do. He had no plan, no idea how he would escape this prison.

As he pushed the down button, a small flicker of a plan came to life in his mind. The doors opened, and he saw a yellow-suited CDC worker standing in the elevator with a sidearm. Kirk glanced at the CDC logo and stepped in.

It took him only a second to size the man up. With

the similar height and weight, Kirk figured he would get one shot at this crazy plan, and this was it. If God was out there, he was throwing him a bone—a very large, yellow bone.

∽∾∾

EVIL AND THE PRESENCE of real power is something that will either scare a host or make it a hopeless addict. Mooch found the feeling of power and the evil that hung inside of him like a dark raging storm cloud to be rather wonderful. He liked the voice and the overpowering urge to want something.

Even though the craving was for blood and murder, it was strong and had a cool feeling that he could not describe. He knew that he was possessed or under some sort of demonic influence, but he didn't care. That was the thing, all he cared about was his next meal—that satisfying meal, and the sound of life as it slipped away.

There is a brief moment when a person dies in which they know the future. The light at the end of the tunnel, or the vision of hell or heaven depending on who owned you, was something that was so pure, so perfect, that the sight of it made Mooch shudder.

It was the look, the way the eyes shadowed over, and as the dying person looked beyond the physical and saw into the ever after, they would transform into their true self. No show, no lies, no best foot forward, but their true, pure self.

How could he stop now? He was, in a way, setting them free, opening them up to the truth and taking away the dross—the blinders people put willingly on as they walk through life. Was it so bad to be true to yourself? Didn't they all say that was the right thing to do, the way to feel real happiness?

Mooch thought of his high school guidance counselor, and the thought occurred to him. He was now doing what they all said people should do. He was being true to himself and doing what he really wanted. He wanted to kill, to take life, and in some way he believed that the lost life was now his, making him stronger. He would not hide it; he would not pretend to be something he was not.

Is this really the result of the teaching of self-love? Is this the way we all should be? He thought, *Yes, this was living—this was the life we should all enjoy. No pretending, just be who you are… yes, and if you wanted to kill or drink beer in church or run around naked, then you should be allowed to do so. Without that freedom, we are all slaves, subject to others and not able to experience life as it was meant to be.*

Mooch closed his eyes, and he squeezed. After he heard the sound of bone snapping, he opened his eyes and looked into the eyes of a beautiful woman. She was so scared, and now as her breath escaped her lungs and the life drained from her, Mooch focused on her eyes.

The spark, the hidden person she hid from the world emerged and he, only he, saw it rise to the surface. He gasped in amazement and smiled.

"I love you, oh how I love you, my sweet Kelli," he whispered. When she heard her name, the little light in her eyes grew to a bright spot, and Mooch pulled her closer so he was only inches from her mouth.

She no longer struggled, her life was slipping, and

any moment Mooch would see what he craved. What *it* craved!

Squeezing harder, Mooch cut off her air supply completely. Not that it mattered. He had slit both her wrists, and the blood loss was taking its toll.

"It's okay, you're free…" Mooch watched, and as Kelli looked beyond him and into the world he knew had to be there, a look of pure horror crossed her face. Mooch looked confused and turned to look at whatever she was staring at. Standing a foot from him, shaded by some unnatural dark force, was a tall, winged thing. It was not only standing behind Mooch, but it was coming *out* of Mooch's body. The long barbed tail hooked around his midsection and the stench that filled the air made Mooch gag.

Dropping Kelli, Mooch screamed and scrambled away on his hands like a crab. The thing took him by the shoulders and forced him back to his task. Mooch grabbed Kelli and finished the job, unable to control his own hands and feet. Weeping, he took one last look into her eyes and saw that now, unlike before, there was nothing.

Dead and dark, the life in her eyes was gone. Mooch looked back over his shoulder and saw nothing but the dingy alley he was kneeling in. Cars passed by just feet from him and the dead girl. He cried and laughed at the same time. It felt so good, and yet he was torn. This was wrong—no, it was right, so right. He was free, free to be…

───※───

EVERY TIME I MADE plans or thought I had *it* all

figured out, something or someone would break into my world and change everything. I was on a mission: find the antidote, save Isis, and recreate the antidote so we could stop the virus. Simple, and yet, here I was sitting in a café, sipping coffee, and staring at a strange man who I was beginning to believe was not what he appeared to be.

The small space that housed the café had big windows facing the street. Small tables ran the length of the windows, and one other row of tables ran down the middle just behind the cash register. One other person sat at a table two down from where we sat, and he was buried in his newspaper and unaware of our presence.

The place was empty, which would seem unnatural, but these days New York was not feeling well. The city had a cold, maybe the flu, so people stayed home, and kids were banned from school until the threat was determined to be gone. A little, gray-haired woman refilled my cup, and I nodded at her. She smiled and gave a warning look to Kreios.

Kreios drank no coffee, but instead sat looking out the window.

"I am a direct man, Mr. Kreios." He turned at the sound of my voice as if he had forgotten I was there. He was so mysterious, and I was burning with questions.

"Kreios. You may call me Kreios."

"Kreios—where to begin? I mean, you healed!" I glanced around, noticing that my voice was too loud. "How did you do that? Who are you, and how do you know who I am? You just walked into the lower levels as if you owned the place… What do you want?" I rattled off my questions like a car salesman going on about the options on the latest SUV.

Kreios stared at me and then said in a calm, powerful voice. "Mark, I know you have questions. I can answer most of them, but some of them will make no sense to you. Some, I will have to show you rather then tell you."

I got the feeling he was asking my permission about something but just leaving out the details of exactly what I was giving him leeway to do.

"I have traveled far to see you, and I believe you have something that belongs to me."

And there it was—he wanted something. "I don't have anything of yours. I've never seen you before." I leaned back in my chair and fiddled with the salt and pepper shakers.

"I am not accusing you of stealing. In fact, I believe you do not even know what it is you have, and no idea it is not yours." He folded his hands and placed them on the table. "But first, we must have a little talk."

I felt like a child sitting in front of the principal. He had this way about him, the way he stood and moved as if he were a thousand years old and this interaction was a pain to him, as if he was far too busy to bother with the likes of me. "Before you go into your little talk, you have to tell me something. How did you heal like that?" I leaned closer, looked into his eyes, and noticed that they were dark, almost black in color.

Kreios touched his neck and sighed. He was a large man, and this sigh made him seem more human. I didn't know why, but I thought of him as something other than human, at least not all human.

"I am not what you think I am. I will not go into that

now, just know that I can heal very fast. If you want to test out your theory and try to kill me, I would urge you not to waste your time. I cannot die, at least not by your hand." I stared at him, and my eyebrows rose.

"Are you telling me that you're immortal? Like some sort of vampire or highlander or something?" My tone was mocking, but somehow I believed him. What was he? His skin was pale, almost white, and he had huge forearms and shoulders. In a fight, I would put my money on him. Not only was he built like a bodybuilder, he was quick and nimble. I'd seen it with my own eyes—he could move like a panther, and for his size, it was crazy.

"In your human terms, yes. I cannot die. Let's just say I am here for two reasons: one is to recover my property, and the other is to stop you from destroying the world."

Just when I was starting to believe this guy, he pulls out that line. I could believe he had a healing power, maybe some experiment or maybe he was like me. I had abilities, well more than just one. I could glimpse into the future and the past, and I could emit some sort of energy out of my body, kind of like a weapon. I did not know what else, and controlling what I knew about was still a learning process.

Kreios looked at me with his dark eyes, and I could see in them the truth. Whatever he was telling me, he believed it to be so. Unwavering and steady. With this, I decided to trust him and go along with his story in order to find out what he was talking about. He knew about me, and I didn't know how much he knew. Did he know about my abilities?

"And why would I want to do that? If you really knew

me, you would know how crazy that statement is. My life is to protect this world, the ones who can't protect themselves. If I am going to destroy the world, I would really like to know how."

Kreios nodded and said. "I know, Mark. You are a good man, you have a kind heart, and I know the last thing you would want to do is destroy the world you try so hard to protect. However, you will do just that if you do not stop."

"Stop what?" I was getting annoyed; he was talking in circles, dodging the real truth. What was so bad that he would travel all this way from wherever he came from just to tell me this?

"Dreaming. You have to stop dreaming."

CHAPTER EIGHT

KREIOS THOUGHT OF HOW to tell Mark Appleton about *who* he was—the right way to break it to the man that he was going to end his own life. He would only tell him what he needed to know, and beyond that, he would just have to come to his own conclusions. He did not want to have to do it like this, but the incident in the WJA's underground center forced his hand.

"What do you mean? How do you—?" Mark looked confused; he stared at the table and took a sip of coffee. His hands were shaking slightly.

"The first thing you must understand is that none of this is your fault. You cannot control your dreams, and for that you are innocent. However, I cannot allow you to keep dreaming, so we must come to some sort of understanding." Kreios had a few ideas. One was to kill Mark even though he believed he was a good man. The other was to find a way to keep him from entering a dream-like state.

Kreios preferred the latter but would do whatever was required of him. In order to dream, a person must enter a second level of sleep. Known by different terms, Kreios knew that if he could train Mark to sleep deeply or maybe drug him to put him so far under that no dream could arise could be a solution. Or he would have to sleep so lightly that any dream would wake him, thus cutting off the result.

"How do I not dream? I take it you know of my ability to see into the future, and just recently, I learned I could see into the past—"

"The past!" Kreios almost stood up, and as he lurched, the table rattled, and Mark's coffee spilled, the warm brown liquid running over the edge and onto the floor. Mark jumped back, dodging the coffee. His eyes flashed and he turned just in time to see the waitress hurry over to clean up the mess.

"Sit down Mark, I got this." Her gray hair was pulled back into a bun, and she had a long apron with a lobster on it that tied in the back. As she wiped up the spilled coffee, she said, "Happens all the time. Just sit down, and I'll get you a fresh cup."

Mark started to protest, but she was already out of sight. The swinging door leading to the kitchen clicked on its hinges.

Kreios settled down, but his face was contorted in what looked like pain. Taking a relaxed posture, he nodded to Mark. "Sorry about that, I was…"

"What is going on? This is ridiculous! You come in our so-called secret building, then I stab you, and you heal. Then you want to take me to coffee and are talking end-of-the-world stuff, and somehow you know all about me and my abilities. I want the truth, no more games. Just be straight up with me." Mark could hear the edge in his voice, but he was tired and frustrated.

Kreios shifted in his seat, and he thought about what Mark said. He knew that whatever he told him would be kept a secret; Mark was a man of secrets.

"I will tell you, but not all at once. It is a lot to take in, so we will start with the important things. First, I am not human, as you might have guessed. I am something else, but what I am is not important. Just know that I am very old, and I will be here long after you are gone. I have abilities as you do. One of them you have seen—I can heal."

"What else can you do?" Mark was getting back into the conversation, and the anger had vanished. The new cup of coffee arrived, and Mark took a sip and smiled up at the waitress.

"I can read minds, and I am very strong." Kreios let a half-smile cross his face as Mark gasped.

"Come on, read minds? That, I don't believe. Strong? Yes, you look it."

"Believe what you will. I am just a small part of this story. You, on the other hand, are the main man, as they say." Kreios folded his hands again and closed his eyes as he searched Mark's memories. He did not see any recollection of his past and decided to move on.

"You have the gifts of *glimpses* and of *energy*. You can harness energy around you and can use it if you so choose. I sense that you have little or no control of this gift." Mark nodded."That's weird, I call them *glimpses,* too. How did you know—" Then a light came on in his eyes. "The mind thing?"

Kreios nodded. "You are a complex man. Even with my ability, I have trouble seeing into your mind because you have different, conflicting memories. This is why I came here, and the reason you and I are here. I know of you, Mark, because you are known to all of my kind. You are taught about, and the story of your life has been told for a thousand years. I know this may be hard to understand, but all I ask is that you trust me. If I tell you one lie, I will leave you and you will never be bothered with me again."

Mark pondered this and said. "How can I trust you? You tell me that you are not even human and that you cannot die. If you lie to me, I'll never know. What if everything you've told me is a lie? For all I know, you just did your research."

"I cannot lie to you because if I did… well, if I lie to you, I will die. My Creator made it so I am unable to lie and live. He is full of love and truth, and a lie is the worst thing one can do, for it saturates the soul—once started, it can never be stopped."

Kreios relaxed his body and held out his hand. He read Mark's thoughts and saw the fear and worry in his heart. But in spite of this, he reached forward and took Mark's hand. The instant they touched, a flash of light filled the room, and the two disappeared.

The man reading the newspaper read on as if he were the only man in the city.

The old woman in the kitchen did not see the two

leave, as she was distracted by handling a book with soft hands. It had come alive the last few days, and the leather cover shimmered as she touched the dark brown skin. She wondered what it was and why nothing was written inside.

"We will find your home, little one. Kirk and that pretty woman will come looking for you soon, don't you worry." She picked it up and put it back in the metal wall safe in the office. After she closed the door and spun the combination, she re-hung the picture and left the office.

<hr>

KIRK WALKED FROM THE hospital dressed in a yellow CDC suit. As he turned the corner, he ran down the back of an alley two blocks from where the hospital was in lockdown. He was amazed how easy it was to leave because of the stupid suit.

He hid the suit under a dumpster—he wanted to keep it just in case he needed to get back into the hospital. Isis was dying, and he would give himself one day to find what he needed. After that, he didn't have a plan. If she died, he didn't know what he would do.

Hang in there, kiddo, just hang in there. The alley was empty, and after he was free of the huge suit, Kirk jogged down to the street and waved down a cab. "The Merc building. Step on it." Taras lived across the street, and Kirk knew that he could get in with his badge. The crime scene was on national news, and the way the terrorist died had the talking heads all in a lather.

"A bomb blew out the entire residence. Police and the FBI are not sure what caused the explosion, but they confirm that Taras Karjanski is dead." It was all the same:

what caused the explosion and who set off the bomb? The WJA and a mention of Mark or Kirk were absent from the news, and as usual they had the story wrong.

The city streets had light traffic, and as the threat of terror heightened, Washington sent in troops. In front of the major government buildings, groups of men stood guard, and a tank or two made the scene surreal.

Who would have thought that we would be guarding our own land with tanks? Kirk shook his head, and as they came to the Merc building, he could see a row of police cars, CDC vans, and other government vehicles parked all around the building. The street was blocked off.

"This is as far as I go, mister, unless you want me to take you around the block to the other side." The cabbie looked over his shoulder. He wore a brown ball cap over dark hair that escaped the cap in thick curls, and he had an unshaven face.

"This is fine," Kirk glanced at the meter and gave the driver a twenty.

"Thanks."

The air was quiet, much too quiet for a downtown street in New York City. It was weird to see this huge city and the tall buildings all but empty. Some people still went into work and did their thing, but most of them decided to stay home.

Kirk closed the door, and the cab took off with a squeal. Walking across the street, he entered the Grove and didn't bother going by the front desk. He took the elevator to the top floor and found the service elevator. He took it up to the floor that Taras Karjanski had turned into a fortress.

"Lot of good that did ya." Kirk muttered. He hated the terrorist and hated even more that he was still killing even after he was dead. What was this world coming to?

Police tape was strung across the opening that used to have doors, and two guards stood wearing dark sunglasses. The closest one stepped forward and put his hand on his piece when he saw Kirk.

"Kirk Weston, Detroit Police Department. I'm working with the FBI on this case." He flashed his badge, and the man took off his glasses and took the identification. He wore a black ball cap, a flak jacket, and combat boots. He did not look like a rent-a-cop; he looked military, maybe ex-military.

"I have no record of you on the list. What do you want here?" His voice was deep, and he looked to be in his late twenties. Kirk tried not to look annoyed but failed. The second retard took a step forward, and Kirk rolled his eyes.

"I'm working on the case and wanted to go over the crime scene one more time—alone, I think better that way, you know, maybe we missed something the first time. Do you want another virus going off in this city, or are you good and comfortable dying of some plague you've never heard of?"

Kirk took his badge back. The two looked at each other and waved him through. He ducked under the tape and gasped. The destruction was more then he remembered. The place looked gutted, and there was a black ring of debris encircling the place where Mark had stood. There was no mistaking where the so-called bomb had gone off.

Looking around, he wondered where Mark was. He

had figured he would be here by now, and the empty floor did nothing to calm Kirk's nerves. *Where are you, Mark?* The lack of the self-appointed superstar made Kirk angry. He was supposed to be here looking for the antidote.

I have to do everything myself. Kirk wondered if Mark would let Isis die. He knew he cared for her, but if he did, then why was he not here looking? Had he already found it and gone?

Charred furniture and broken glass littered the room. Kirk walked through and began searching each room. One by one, he discovered nothing of any use. A wall safe, open and empty. A hidden floor safe, and it, too, was open and empty.

He cursed and spit, and taking a broken bottle of Vodka, he tipped it back and downed the rest in one gulp. It burned as it went down, and Kirk squinted and grimaced. "Got to give it to the Russians, they sure do make good booze." Tossing the bottle to the ground, he smiled when it shattered.

Something that Mark said on the phone reminded Kirk that there was another floor, some sort of command center or computer room. Kirk didn't find any stairwell or hidden passage, so he left and gave the two guards a nod and a grunt as he passed under the police tape.

Taking the elevator down one floor, he got off and walked down the hall, noticing the doors on each side of the hallway. They were numbered, most were apartments, and in the middle on the left hand side, Kirk saw one that had no number, and the door was made of metal instead of wood like the others.

Kirk put his ear to the door and listened. All was quiet

on the other side. He pulled out a thin wire-like device he had taken from the WJA weapons room. It was a fiber optic camera, and on the other end was a small screen. Kirk slid the tiny camera under the door and turned his attention to the screen.

He controlled the camera and saw that this indeed was some kind of computer room. Twinkling lights and flashing green LED lights cut through the dark room. Kirk turned the camera and scanned the left and then the right. The room looked deserted.

Retracting the cable, he slid the compact device back into his pocket. He tried the door, and it was locked. Stepping back, he flexed his right leg, and with all his force, he kicked the door. The sound of metal grinding filled the empty hall.

Kirk felt the vibrations run up his leg and to his skull. The door didn't budge. Taking a second step back, he rushed the door with his shoulder down. The door flexed just a little, and yet remained. Kirk muttered a curse and rubbed his shoulder. It ached. Kirk stared at the forbidding door, and he rubbed his head, which was not as smooth as he liked to keep it

He could feel his anger rise, and his face felt hot. With hands quivering, he turned, searching for something to hit or kick. He flexed his back and his vision blurred as he ground his teeth and cried out.

Ten feet away, a fire extinguisher hung in a case imbedded in the wall. The glass door read, "Break in case of emergency." Kirk close fisted the glass, and it shattered. He grabbed the red fire extinguisher and ran to the door, still hot as ever.

Taking the butt of the heavy, metal tank, he bashed the doorknob repeatedly. The metal knob bent, and after the fifth or sixth hit, the knob gave away and fell to the floor. This time, the kick to the door had a better result. It flew open and slammed against the wall on the other side.

Stepping into the darkness, Kirk walked toward the wall of computers. The place hummed with machinery. Kirk felt for the light switch, and as the light came on, he saw that this was not only a computer room, but a storage facility. Tall, walk-in coolers stood against the east wall, and a biohazard symbol marked the doors of each.

"What do we have here?" Kirks heart skipped a beat. *Could it be this easy?*

CHAPTER NINE

TAKING A BOTTLE OF scotch from the bar in the far corner of his office, the president poured the dark liquor into a crystal glass. He tipped it back and winced as it burned its way down his throat. He poured more, took the glass, walked to the couch, and sat down with a sigh.

The stock market had taken a huge hit, and the tailspin didn't look like it would pull up any time soon.

The president rubbed his chin and looked at the reports. The thing of it was that he had no idea how to save the country he loved. The last moron who held his office took them lower than anyone ever thought possible, and he was left to clean up his mess.

And now this! Oil was in high demand, and even with the oil credits, the people were in an outrage. Riots and looters filled the streets, and the military wanted him to declare martial law, but he wanted to hold off as long as he could. Once that hammer came down, things could grow beyond his grip in a hurry. He did dispatch the military to government buildings and the virus sites in New York, but that was the extent of it.

Schools were still closed, and as people stayed home from work, the flow of money that kept their economy going all but stopped.

What am I going to do? We are beyond repair. We can't drill fast enough to fix the gas shortage. The country, and now the world, is at a standstill because of this Karjanski mess. Now they all are looking to me for the answers. I've got none, nothing but the truth. And the truth is—we are about to see the end of the United States of America.

"FINISH THE JOB! TAKE this country—no, take the world down and feel the power of God like never before." Mooch stared at the computer screens in front of him. The voice in his head made his skin crawl.

Never before had he felt this way—so full, so free. It was like that feeling on a rollercoaster just before you drop, the excitement and the fear. He knew that the things he would do to Kirk Weston were only the beginning. He knew he could do so much more, be so much more.

"Hold on to your so-called free world. We are about to see what happens when you lose everything." The stock market was online and almost everything was controlled by a computer somewhere. Typing on the keys with cat-like speed, Mooch pulled up the New York Stock Exchange website. Hacking in took over an hour, but soon he was in full control. Before he did what he wanted to do, Mooch linked the site with a timer and set the clock for noon tomorrow.

After he was done, he logged into the utilities network—gas, power, electric and water. All were controlled by one main government site, and even though most believed that each individual company handles their own utilities, the truth was that the government had the on and off switch to the whole ball of wax.

With this power at his fingertips, Mooch sat back, took a long swig of Dr Pepper, and threw the empty can over his shoulder. He could now control the flow and the price of everything. Not like it would matter. By noon tomorrow, money would mean nothing.

Checking his own bank account, he smiled at the amount that showed up on the screen. Not only did he have a few million, but the majority of it was in gold. Taking a piece of paper out of his desk, he wrote a note to himself.

Buy food and supplies.

After setting his mom's house on fire, he left and took the time to set up his new base of operation. Mooch then set up his office and made sure he could survive in his hideout for a year. All he was lacking was the food.

He picked up his cell phone and dialed a food delivery service. He ordered two truckloads of food, most of it canned and dried. He placed the order for 10 a.m. the following day.

"You sure you want all this stuff?" The man on the other end said.

"Yes, I am a survivalist, and I am in the stocking mode of my year. Just be here on time."

"Okay… whatever you say."

Mooch hung up and went back to his computer. Next was the Transportation Department. He opened a fresh can of Dr Pepper and took a sip. It was going to be fun to see the world burn.

———∞∞∞———

WHAT DOES IT FEEL like to travel in between dimensions or to stop time? We as a human race can only detect and study 4 percent of all matter and energy. Dark Energy and the invisible take up the other 96 percent, about which we are clueless. But we understand that what lies beyond our sight and our own understanding is, in essence, more real then what we can see, feel, taste, and hear.

All at once for me, the ideas of time travel, teleportation, telekinesis, and other phenomena were not just written in books or played out on the big screen. What if they are real? It is believed that there are eleven to twenty-two other dimensions, and maybe more. What if the world we know and love is not even real compared to the unseen. What if the invisible look at us with wonder at our ignorance and pride? Could we even learn beyond our own mental walls? We are imprisoned by the very ideas that make us free.

All these thoughts came crashing through my thick head as I touched Kreios's hand. He closed his eyes, and as the world stopped, I looked at the frozen man with his newspaper, and the door to the kitchen had stopped mid-swing.

The café seemed to age, and as I watched, the floor changed and the color of the walls went from a light blue to a bright red. The barstools and counter that wrapped around morphed into a modern bar top that curved to make a U-shape.

I blinked, and when I opened my eyes, I was no longer in the café but standing in someone's home. Kreios stood next to me, and without a word, he walked to the fireplace and picked up a picture frame. I followed, still in a fog, as I tried to figure out what was happening to me.

"Mark, this house is a thin place; the café is also a thin place, and somehow the worlds and the fabric that holds them together are torn and about to break down altogether." He handed me the photograph, and I looked into my own eyes.

It was a picture of me. I was standing in front of a big oak tree, and the tall green grass behind me gave the photo warmth. Next to me, holding my hand, was a woman. Not K, but someone else. Sitting in the grass at our feet was a little boy. He was two, maybe three years old, and his blond hair stuck up in the same weird way mine did.

My heart beat faster, and all of the sudden, my mouth was dry. I licked my lips, tore my focus from the photograph, and tried to ask Kreios a question. There was only one real question, but all that came out of my mouth was a grunt. I looked back down to the photo, and Kreios put his hand on my shoulder.

"What you must be thinking… I know that you are used to this kind of thing, but somehow this particular place is different." He took a deep breath and let it out slowly. "Try not to think too hard about it. Things will go much better if you just go with it and try to learn what you must. We all have troubles and trials in our lives. Yours are just—well… different."

I cleared my throat and managed a question. "When is this place? Is it real or a glimpse?"

Kreios shook his head. "I can't tell you that. You need to find the truth, and you need to do it fast. Our world depends on you, and I am not going to let you destroy everything because of your ignorance." He had a hint of anger laced in his voice. I turned when I heard someone come in from the next room.

It was my kitchen; I knew it was even though this house was new to me. Yet at the same time, it was familiar. How could it feel so new and old at the same time? And what was he talking about, saying that this was a thin place? I could not deny that, at times, this life felt paper-thin, but that was just a way of describing how fake some things felt.

"Mark… home so soon? You look tired, are you okay?" A thin, dark haired woman reminded me of someone I used to know, but her name escaped me. I was in shock, or maybe I wasn't letting my mind open up to this reality.

"I… uh—I had—" I stuttered and looked back to Kreios, but to my surprise, he was gone. Vanished as if I had dreamed him up. Now as I stood looking at this woman who seemed to know me, I felt love toward her and wondered how I ended up here.

The woman took my hand in hers and pulled me close as she kissed me. I could feel my face flush; the feeling of passion and the need to be loved and held by this person flooded my body and soul. "I'm not complaining—I was hoping you would come home early. I missed you."

Was she aware of my glimpses? Had I been gone for a long time? I held her at arm's length and looked into her eyes, and in a half second, the memories of my other life took over—my job with the WJA, the bombing, my tears at K and Sam's death, revenge, and the wedding that followed a year-and-a-half later. The birth of my son... Samson—we named him Samson.

I felt hot tears fill my eyes as the emotions of who was standing in front of me hit me for the first time. It was Maria, sweet Maria. She helped me to get over K and loved me for who I was in spite of my pain and shortcomings. How could I have ever forgotten her?

The old memories still were there, but these new ones were so much stronger. They were so full and powerful that the idea of K and Sam in my other life seemed as if *it* was all a dream. But in the background, I knew that they were not a dream, this was the dream. Kreios had somehow sent me here to show me something. But what?

"Maria," Just saying her name sent a shiver up my spine. "I missed you, too." Her eyes lit up, and the spark of love I had for her exploded in my heart. Had I loved her all along? Even with K being alive and finding out that my life with Maria was just a dream did not take away all my feelings for her. It was real to me, and how I ever forgot her was beyond me.

"I love you, Mark, more then you will ever know." She kissed me again, and this time, I took her in my arms and drank in her love. Maria, our conversations in the middle of the night, long walks, and just holding her and smelling her hair consumed my mind. Flashes of memories took over as I kissed her.

My head hurt, and my lower back ached as I began to think of K and Sam. They were at home, and now as I held Maria, guilt hit me. How could I love two women at the same time? One was real, and one was just in my dreams.

But as soon as the guilt began to creep up in my heart, I remembered all the memories of my life with Maria. We had a child, a boy. How could I have this memory of a life with her and it be a dream? I had to test it and find out if this was the real world, or one in my head. If this was real, then my wife and daughter were dead, and I was a father of a son. But if not, I was a cheating husband, even if just in my dreams.

CHAPTER TEN

KREIOS OPENED HIS EYES and took the hot cup of coffee from across the table. He could smell the roast, the aroma of the beans.

His head pounded as the call of the book accosted his nerves and senses. It was close, maybe even in this very café. He could feel it. As he finished Mark's coffee, he watched the older woman come up to his table and give him a quizzical look.

"Your friend had to go?" She looked toward the door and then back at him.

"Yes, he had somewhere to be." Picking up her thoughts, he lowered his eyebrows and took her hand. She started to pull away, but as soon as she saw his dark eyes begin to lighten and then glow with bright light, she relaxed.

"You have something that belongs to me." His voice was low and strong.

Shaking her head, she paused with a knowing look, and then nodded her head up and down as she changed her mind. "I think I do... yes, the book... it's yours. Take it, I am scared of it. It's not of this world, am I right?" Her hand shook a little and Kreios smiled.

"You are right, my sweet child. It is a personal book, and I would love to have it returned to me. I have been searching for a long time, and knowing that it will soon be home and that such a wonderful woman has taken care of it all this time brings comfort to my soul."

The face of the old woman beamed with the complement. She blushed a deep shade of red, and Kreios stood up, still holding her hand. Leading her back to the kitchen, he released her and watched with interest as she took a painting off the wall in her office and worked the combination on a wall safe.

"Someone left it here last week. I was keeping it for them, and I thought your friend might know who it belonged to. The pretty woman who was with this other bald man—Kirk, I think his name was—left it here. Then there was that explosion across the street, and the virus scare." She blubbered on. Kreios knew that she was nervous.

"This whole world is going to hell. I knew this book was special the moment I laid my eyes on it." Her voice softened as she took it out and held it close to her chest. "I knew with all the excitement, it was just overlooked, but they would have come back for it eventually." She eyed him.

"This is yours. I can feel it somehow, as if it wants to be with you. Is that crazy?" She hugged the book tighter and stepped toward him as if he were a principal and she was just a student looking for approval.

"I thank you for keeping it safe. You will be looked after, I will make sure of it. May I?" Kreios held out his hand, and she handed him the book. A line of regret formed in her forehead. Kreios took the book and looked down at it, running a finger over the rough, leather cover.

"Well—" The old woman breathed in a sigh of relief and put her hands on her hips. "Glad that is over... I was afraid of what it might do if I kept it any longer." Her face gave away to a large grin.

Kreios smiled at her, and the look this time did not seem odd for his face but was true and natural. This book, the return of it, made him happy. "I am in your debt."

"Think nothing of it, was the least I could do. Just don't lose it again, I have a feeling that thing in the wrong hands could do something terrible." She marched back out of the office and ushered Kreios out of the kitchen. "Thank you for taking it off my hands. I wanted to keep it but didn't want to at the same time... you know what I mean?"

"I do. It has a way of holding the keeper in a trance. Much longer, and I may have had to take it from you by force." The old woman nodded as if she understood. Kreios thanked her again and left the café.

Mission one accomplished. Now to deal with Mark. What must he be thinking? Kreios turned down an alley behind the café. The light from the sun was blocked by concrete and brick, so even in the daytime the alley was dark and gloomy. A dumpster and garbage rotting gave it a rank smell, but none of this bothered Kreios. He had his book back, and that was all that mattered.

Finding a spot to sit, Kreios looked around and made sure that he was alone. It seemed that even the street people were in hiding these days. The alley was empty, so he unlatched the metal buckles and opened the book to somewhere in the center. The page was blank, like all the other pages, but as soon as Kreios touched the parchment with his fingers, words appeared in a scrawling script. They glowed in the dim light, and Kreios felt his heart jump in his chest.

THE ROOM FELT COOL as the raised floor cooled from below and made a circular motion throughout the room in order to keep the machines from overheating. Air moved through the small holes in each floor tile and went up and into the air ducts above and back around again.

Kirk wondered why the police had not discovered this room yet. Maybe they thought everything Taras owned was on the floor he lived in. This didn't surprise Kirk in the least. The NYPD were overworked, and most of the time it was a battle between them and the Feds. Their little turf war seemed more important than actual police work.

At the far end of the room, three, tall coolers stared at Kirk as if to warn him not to enter. Leaving was not an option, so Kirk took hold of a cold, silver handle and pulled. The middle cooler hissed as the door opened with reluctance. Freezing air washed into the room, and a fog rolled along the floor like some kind of monster.

Kirk flipped the light switch mounted on the outside of the cooler, and a single bulb flickered and came on.

"Here goes nothing."

Floor-to-ceiling racks took up the left and the right side of the cooler. The room was ten feet tall and twenty feet long. Kirk looked up to find that the room had three light bulbs. The other two were burnt out.

Kirk could feel the freezing air begin to work its way through his clothes, and at the far end of the room, an air conditioning unit kicked on and blasted more chilled air into the cooler. Taking a few steps into the room, Kirk scanned the racks, which were filled with canisters that looked like small, silver thermoses. He picked up the nearest one and read the label.

The writing was in Russian, or what looked like Russian to Kirk. He saw the clear biohazard symbol and picked up another one and saw that it was the same. *How am I supposed to find the antidote if they are all in Russian?*

Turning to the rack on the left, he took a canister and saw that this one was in French. He knew the look and recognized a word. The word, "warning" wasn't hard to recognize no matter what language it was written in.

The magnitude of what Kirk was seeing hit him. This was his storehouse, his chemical warfare stockpile. How many countries had he had this stuff made in? Looking down the rows of coolers, he wondered if the other two were the same.

Leaving the middle cooler, Kirk opened the door to the cooler on the far right. This one looked the same, racks filled with canisters, but most of these were labeled in some Middle Eastern dialect.

Cooler number three was locked. Kirk went into the

hall, grabbed the fire extinguisher, and bashed the handle until it fell off with a clatter. He smiled and pulled the cooler door open. This one was different, not different in size or shape, but in the contents. Frozen bodies hung from large hooks. Their faces, stilled and cold, stared at him.

Kirk took a step backward and held his breath. No stench lingered because of the frozen climate. He breathed in and took a closer look.

In two rows, twenty-five bodies, most of them men, hung. He found one woman and a teenage boy that looked to be fifteen or so. All were missing limbs, fingers, and other parts Kirk would not want to go without.

Kirk looked for the missing parts but didn't find them. He scanned each face to see if any of them were familiar to him. They all were nameless faces and didn't bring to mind anyone he might know.

The freezing air made Kirk shiver and his teeth chatter. He left the room and shut the door, jamming the broken handle into the seam to keep the door closed. He didn't want this cooler to thaw out.

The hum of computers and the rattle of the air conditioners gave the room an industrial feel. Kirk took a seat on the floor and rubbed his head. He was on an emotional rollercoaster and he was not used to having these feelings. Isis was dying, he had found nothing he could use, and Mark was missing. He was pissed, sad, and hurt. He was not one to be hurt, and the feeling reminded Kirk of why he had closed himself off to the world.

"Mark, where are you?" He cursed and looked up at the wall of monitors. He listened to the sound of the machines. He needed Mooch. He could crack into these things and tell him where to find the antidote. But Mooch was dead.

———✇———

CHEATER, LIAR, DEADBEAT, LOSER, lost, confused, mixed up, alone, in love, hopeful, and *so* going to die. These words all ran through my mind and filtered down into my gut in a hard ball of worry. K was home with my daughter, Sam, wondering where I was, hoping I was okay, and worrying that I might not ever come home because I might have a bullet in my head.

I was in my other home, holding another woman. Not only that, but I had made a child with this woman—a little boy whom I loved just as much as I loved Sam. Maria filled my heart just as much as K did. My heart and brain split down the middle, and the ball turned over in my stomach, making me want to die.

What was I doing? Did I think this was okay? How could it be? But if I was with K, I was cheating on Maria; when I was with Maria, I was cheating on K.

"What's wrong? You seem tense." Maria looked at me with her brown eyes, so deep and powerful. She kissed me on the nose, and I shook my head.

"I'm just tired. It's been a long day." I could feel my heart swell as I looked at her. My God, she was so beautiful, so perfect and fragile. I pulled her close, breathed in her scent, and buried my face in her neck.

"You don't seem tired to me…" She giggled and wriggled in my arms. "I think you need some mommy-daddy time." She freed herself, took my hand, and pulled me toward the stairs.

Big butterflies leapt in my stomach, and I let her lead me to my dreams and to my doom. Torn between reality and imagination, I asked her something I knew would kill the mood. I was a master at killing the mood.

"Do you remember K?"

Maria stopped dead and the look of playfulness vanished. She studied me and saw in my face that this was not a joke. "Yes, how could I forget?"

"Was I married to her? Did she die in an explosion?" I wanted to know what time and world I was in. What had Kreios done to me?

"Mark, why are you doing this to yourself? You did nothing wrong. They died, you avenged their deaths, and now you have a new life. With me and Samson." Her eyes showed the hurt I was inflicting.

"I'm sorry, I just feel like I will forget them one day, and wake up to find myself without all the people I love. It feels like it was just yesterday…"

Maria took my hand again, and I followed her. She knew just how to comfort me, just what to say. She understood the pain I was in. But the me she knew was not the me I was, or was the me I thought I was just all in my head?

Kreios told me that I was doing something that could hurt us all. Something that, when I dreamed, was going to destroy us, or me, or maybe everything. I knew if this kept up and I had to keep tearing my heart, I wouldn't recover from it.

Was I really in some other world, an alternate universe? I scoffed at the idea, but something was going on. I was somehow walking into another life, and it was real. How can I have memories and a family and remember getting married and having a child with Maria if it's just a dream?

I needed to find Kreios and make him tell me what was going on. He was something other than human, and if he was just in my head, was my life with K the dream? I could only think of one way to know for sure. I had to dream, and if I could dream, then it was real. I knew that I couldn't glimpse inside of a glimpse.

One way or another, I was going to find out where and when I was… or end up in a straight jacket and a padded room.

CHAPTER ELEVEN

KREIOS STARED, AND HIS lips parted just a little as the words on the page moved, and in a way, wrote themselves. The letters appeared one at a time and made up words. The words were the exact story of Kreios's life.

Kreios knew that, in the wrong hands, his life would be in danger. This was *his* book, the Book of Life for his soul, and it recorded in every detail who he was, all his thoughts and feelings down to the smallest little thing. This book kept notes and changed from moment to moment.

Shutting the book, he latched each buckle and made sure they were locked in place. He could feel his life force pulse in rhythm with the heart of the book. Everyone of his kind had a book like this, but for a human each book was stored in the third heaven under the guard. These things were beyond explanation.

This *Book of Kreios* was no longer safe behind tall, thick doors and guarded by inhuman beasts, but free to be taken and destroyed, which would condemn Kreios to hell along with his brothers. He was not of this world, and he knew that now that he had possession of the book—his book—once again, he would not let it out of his sight ever again.

Holding the thick book to his chest, he chanted something in another tongue, and the large, leather bound work shivered and began to shrink. It grew smaller and soon was the size of a saltine cracker. Kreios placed in a soft leather wrap and tucked it into his pocket.

He wanted to eat it, for that was the only way to keep it completely safe, but he feared what it might do to him if he turned against his Creator once again. His shame and guilt hounded him, and he vowed years ago never to betray again. It was an evil world, and there were people all around this land that would kill, rape, and deceive to get what they wanted, but Kreios was not one of them. He was true and righteous in every way.

Looking up at the sun, high in the sky, he marveled at the way these people built so high and strong. Buildings of metal and glass towered over the street, and yet the long, trash-littered streets were void of the normal crowds.

News of bombs, terrorists, and a virus kept most indoors. Now, as the country crumbled under its own fear, the forces Kreios knew of took flight, laughed, and mocked, as the once powerful human race began to destroy itself.

"Dust to dust, ashes to ashes." Kreios said under his breath. It was a sad thing, and even in this world, he hoped that he could prevent the end by killing one man.

Mark Appleton.

"Time to see what he thinks of his new life."

———— ∞∞∞ ————

I COULD FEEL SOMETHING tug at my sleeping brain.
A glimpse, a dream. I had one. How could I have one here
in this world and still have one in the world with K and
Sam? This made no sense, and yet, here I was.

It was dark in the house, and the only sounds of life
came from Maria, who slept soundly, breathing in and out
with deep sighs that on any other night would seem sweet.
I could hear Samson down the hall, as he breathed a little
louder and made a nice racket that his wife one day would
appreciate.

The air was cool and the moon cast a soft blue and
white light across the floor at the foot of the bed. I pulled
off the covers, slipped to my feet, and left the bedroom
without a sound.

In this world, I also worked for the WJA. After my
wife and daughter were killed, I found the men who did
the bombing and killed them all in a cabin just outside of
the city. I remembered Isis following me and introducing
me to Solomon and the rest of the team. Big B and
Jamison, all of them were still alive, and no terrorist
named Taras Karjanski or the Red Dog ever did anything.
This was a different outcome to a life or a choice made.
I chose to love Maria and to move on after my family's
death. I chose to be a killer and to fight for justice.

Now here in this place, I didn't know what to think
or what to do. This was real, but so was my other life.
I couldn't understand how that could be, but I was not
just going off of feelings but the test. I couldn't have

a glimpse, or a dream within a dream. But here I was, dreaming inside what I thought was a dream.

The kitchen was bathed in the same calming light, and I looked out over the backyard. I took a deep breath in and let it out slowly.

"How is Maria?" The sound startled me, and that was not an easy thing to do. I was a trained assassin; I could hear the tiniest sound and could somehow feel if another person entered the room. Kreios looked at me with a nondescript expression.

My heart rattled in my chest, my palms were all of a sudden wet with perspiration. "Beautiful as ever." I was not happy to see him because his presence meant that I was going back under or coming out of whatever I was in, and I wasn't sure how I felt about that.

"Why are you doing this to me? Do you like to mess with my head, to tear my heart out, making me choose between K and Maria?"

Kreios took a step toward the end of the counter and placed his hand on the cool, granite top. "I am not doing anything. This is your world, your mistake, and your mess. This is what you create every time you dream." He stared at me with dark, almost black eyes. I wondered again what he was.

"What are you talking about? I am not doing anything. I can't help dreaming, it just happens. You think I like this power or ability? You think I like to have these memories and these feelings toward two women, having children one of whom I have to watch die and knowing that the other will never see me again?" My blood began to boil. I was confused and not in the mood for games. I needed answers; I needed to know what this was—this place, and this time.

"Sit down, we need to talk. I was hoping you would figure this out on your own, but I see you are emotional and not in your right mind." His voice was sharp, and I had to hold back from decking him. It would feel good to smash his face and see him bleed. Not that it would do any good, the guy healed amazingly fast. Too fast.

I pulled up a barstool and sat down, eyeing him. I wanted him to know that I was not happy, not glad to be here, and not glad to see him.

"I know you are not happy, not glad to see me."

Oh, right, the mindreading thing.

"Mark, some of your abilities, you are still unaware of. One is your sixth sense, as you call it, the ability to feel danger, almost as if you know where it is coming from. It gives you an advantage in battle."

I thought back over the many battles I had been in and knew that he was telling the truth. I could somehow predict what the other person was going to do before they did it. I was glad I could because it kept me alive.

"Your glimpses are not what you think they are. You think that they are looks into the future, a kind of time travel, or a way to see the future or the past. This idea is sort of right, but wrong in all the ways that are important." Kreios sighed as if telling me something simple, and as if I were so stupid that he had to spell it out for me.

"They are not the future, they are not the past. They are a creation." At this, I opened my mouth but nothing came out. He waited and looked at me, and I knew he was doing it again.

What do you mean, "a creation"? I am just looking into the future... I only did the past thing one time, and I had to try hard. It wasn't easy.

"I know, but what you are doing every time you dream is creating a new world, an alternate universe, if you will. The things you see are the beginning of a new existence, and each world starts with you in that exact moment. You set in motion a chain of events, and just because they apply to you in your world does not mean they are not real.

You see, this world you are in right now is a creation, a new dimension. Maria and Samson and you are real now, but did not exist before you dreamed them. The family and the memories, once you stepped over, are all just as real as your life with K and Sam."

I felt lightheaded, and all at once, the room began to spin. How could this be, it was impossible. Kreios stepped forward, steadied me, and asked me if I was okay. I couldn't speak, so he took a glass, filled it with water from the tap, and handed it to me. My life and what I believed was real now was something different altogether.

"Mark, I know that you did not know what you were doing, but now that you do, you must stop. You have created hundreds of worlds. Each version is now real, and all of them will converge and destroy the key world. There can only be twelve dimensions, or the whole thing falls apart."

"Twelve! What are you talking about? There can't be twelve." I couldn't wrap my brain around what Kreios was saying.

"Yes, but the Creator only made this universe to hold

twelve, and we are now in the hundreds thanks to you. I am here to stop you and help you to fix this mess before He sends something much more evil to do it for you. There are beings you cannot imagine, creatures you never want to meet."

I took a sip of the cold water and placed the glass on the counter. "What can I do? I don't even know how or what I am doing, so how can I stop something I can't even control?" I knew that this had to be true, but I still couldn't keep from shaking. My hands trembled, and the memories of K and Maria fought inside my head. Now I knew why this felt real—both were real—but what did that mean?

"What do you mean, the 'key world'? Is there one that is more real than the other?"

Kreios nodded. "Yes, but the problem is that the key world is moving. This is the main reason I am here."

"What do you mean, 'moving'? How can it move?"

Kreios took a hold of my shoulders and looked me in the eyes. His stare unnerved me to my core. "It is moving because the key world is the one you are in. When you move to another world, it moves with you."

BILL MALONE STOOD AT his desk overlooking the floor of the New York Stock Exchange. He loved his job. The feeling and the action made him feel like God. The power of his position was intoxicating.

He scanned the bank of computer monitors in front of him and kept a watchful eye on the numbers at the lower right hand corner of the screens. These were the totals, the end numbers, the ones that mattered. Ten-thousand seemed to be the key, the number that made the people calm and kept them buying and spending to the limit on their credit cards.

Everything had taken a dip with the recent terrorist threat and the bombings of some oil refineries, but it was still holding steady. Bill didn't have kids, so the school scare did nothing for him. The government caught the guy, and he was dead.

He watched again as the numbers fell with news of a virus on the loose in New York, but not as much as he expected. Things were good, business as usual.

A bell sounded, but in his soundproofed room, the main floor and all the noise that came along with it were silenced. The alarm that sounded in the room itself was a bell that Bill did not ever want to hear. It meant that the numbers took a sharp enough dip that it was worth worrying about, worth calling a few people that had a lot of investments and would pay him well to give them advanced warning.

The mug of scalding coffee—he liked it scalding—fell from his grip, clipped the edge of the counter that held the bank of monitors and spun end over end, throwing scalding coffee all over the front of Bill's cream-colored slacks.

Bill felt the searing liquid soak through his pants, and he jumped back with a yelp. The mug hit the floor and shattered, sending a single piece of pottery into Bill's shin. It cut through his slacks and dug in a half-inch into his flesh.

But Bill did not scream out because of the hot coffee burning his crotch or the piece of ceramic coffee mug sticking into his shin. He screamed out in pain because of the numbers at the bottom of the monitors.

The numbers were all at zero. Every last one of them. Bill regained his balance and looked down to the floor, and even though he couldn't hear anything beyond his sealed office, he could feel the air, taste the tension.

His vision blurred as stars blinked across his eyes. He fainted and fell backward. He hit the floor hard, his head crushing what was left of the coffee mug, and another sharp piece of ceramic dug into the back of his skull.

Bill would not be waking up. He didn't die from the shin wound or the wound to the back of his head. He died from the heart attack.

CHAPTER TWELVE

KIRK STOMPED HIS FEET and muttered a string of curses. The floor made a hollow sound as the empty space underneath echoed. He stood up and walked to the wall of monitors. He found a keyboard and began hitting random keys, not sure what he expected but just frustrated that he felt all but worthless.

"Stupid computers, they're all the same…" The screen didn't change, and he picked up the keyboard and threw it down. The plastic shattered when it hit the floor and black plastic pieces flew in all directions.

Kirk could feel the heat in his face and neck as rage filled his blood stream. Shaking, he gripped the edge of the nearest monitor and tore it from the wall. With a mighty heave, he tossed it against the far wall, and it burst into pieces and exploded.

Breathing heavily, Kirk balled his fists, and with a right hook, he drove his fist into the wall. Drywall and paint chips flew, and he yanked his hand free, not caring that he could have broken it.

"It's not fair!" He screamed.

Sitting on the floor, he saw a computer tower. It was black with a few red lights flashing, and just the sight of it enraged Kirk even more. He took hold of the devil box and pulled. The thing was heavy, much too heavy to be a computer. Tugging and working his back muscles, he managed to drag it out from under the countertop.

Turning it over, he ripped the cords from the back and one of the monitors went black. This made him feel better almost immediately.

Something was not right with this box. It was smooth and felt cold. Most towers were hot or warm—not cold. He worked his fingers under the thin plastic shell—pulled and strained to break the casing from tiny screws that held it in place.

The box was not giving Kirk what he wanted. Kirk took out his service weapon and fired three times at the edge of the box. Plastic splintered and broke away. This made Kirk half smile. The sound of the gun and the smell of gunpowder also lowered his rage level.

"You will not win. This is my house—" Kirk got down on his hands and knees and ripped the broken shell from the tower. Under the husk of black plastic was a silver box. Not a computer at all but some sort of safe—or a cooler.

Excitement filled Kirk with hope as he turned the box on end so the front looked up at him. There was a small, electronic key pad. The small screen was lit up in green even though all known power was no longer attached to the device.

Looking at the key pad for a moment Kirk thought of all the possible combinations. There were endless possibilities. Too many to try to guess. He was going to have to bypass the door, maybe by force. Only problem was, this box seemed to have no seams or joints. As if it were made of a single, solid piece of metal.

Only one thing to do. Take it with me and try to figure out how to get inside. Maybe Mark could help, if only Mark were around.

The thought made Kirk angry again. Here he was trying to save Isis's life, and Mark was out doing whatever he was doing. Whatever it was, he wasn't saving Isis. He was MIA.

MOOCH ALLOWED A GRIN to cross his face as he watched the stock market crash. Not that it mattered, money was worthless, of no value now. The only thing that would be worth anything by this time next week would be food and guns.

Money would hold no value if all the people wanted was a meal. Trading and working to keep what you had were soon to be a thing of the past. Gold, silver, who cared? It was just a piece of metal—worthless trinkets compared to water, food, heat, and a gun to defend what you had.

Tanks of fuel and backup generators stood in a line fifty feet behind Mooch's office. This next phase would be the killer. Without power, the world would fall in 24 hours. He didn't care about all the people that were going to die. Couldn't care less about the hospitals whose backup generators would soon run low on fuel, and whatever and whoever they were keeping alive died off like so many cattle.

Mooch would find a willing woman, maybe two, and start over. He would run things, and he alone would be the god of this world. Take that!

———∞∞∞———

THE POP OF BREAKERS made Kirk jump. He had the box in his arms and was about to lug it back to the Merc building when he heard the sound and all the lights went off. Leaning and setting the box down, he looked back into the silent room. The absence of noise made his skin crawl.

No hum of machines, no grind of air conditioners. He could hear faint screams coming from the other rooms. Kirk listened and waited for the backup generators to kick on, but none did. His mind went to the three large coolers. To the bodies that soon would begin to thaw out, and with them, the smell of dead flesh. He then thought of the vials of who-knows-what began to thaw as well. The thought made Kirk swallow hard. His mouth and throat went dry, and it felt like he just ate a handful of cotton balls.

He remembered what Mark told him: how the virus became lethal when it was above 32 degrees. He took one last look at the room and listened to the popping sound as the coolers began to warm up. It was the sound of death, the sound of the end.

Kirk grunted, picked up the box, and pushed the elevator button. He wondered how long they had. No thought of trying to keep the stockpile cold, no misguided ideas of saving the world. All Kirk wanted was to save Isis, to save the woman he loved.

Chapter Thirteen

HOW DOES ONE STOP dreaming? How can I force myself to sleep yet not dream? I drank the rest of the water in my glass and sighed. I knew that this information was crazy, but my life seemed to be a string of crazy and unexplained events.

Kreios looked at me and I could see the wheels turning. He had a plan but for some reason wasn't going to tell me. Maybe he would kill me, was that the only real answer?

"So, what happens when I leave? Is there another me running around with Kirk and K over on the other side?" I didn't think so; someone would have noticed… maybe I stopped time on the other worlds.

"In a way." Kreios paced the floor and the soft light of the moon streaming in through the kitchen window made his hair look white, almost unreal as if *he* were not real. Was Kreios someone I made up, a figment of my imagination?

"A version of you is still there but you are asleep, in a dream, and to you, time is moving very slow. Just as hundreds of other versions of you are living out their lives in real time in other universes. The last one you were in is the only one that will be in slow motion, but that will only last so long. As time goes by, if you stay here, the other world will speed up, and real time will continue. You cannot occupy more than one place at a time."

"Let me get this straight. I am sitting in a café or lying on my bed in that other world, and at the same time, I am in a hundred or so other places going about my life, unaware of this and what is going on?" My head began to throb.

Kreios nodded. "Yet they are not you. They were you but now are making their own decisions independent of you altogether. If you enter their world, you become them just as you became this copy. That is why you remember his memories, his life, or the life you could have had."

This caught me off guard. "You mean this isn't my life? What is my real life then?"

"That is for you to decide."

"Come on, that's a lame, Yoda-like answer. Just tell me—where is my first life, the one I *should* be living?" I could feel deep resentment welling up in my gut. "How do you know you are talking to the real me? I could be just the copy, or one of a hundred other copies of the same person."

"This is you. I found you, and because you are the only one who can dream and create a new world, I know you are the one who can stop this madness." Kreios grunted and his voice was harsh. I could see his frustration, and I wondered how he came to have this task of stopping me, a fool who didn't even know what he was doing.

"Okay, so how do we fix this? I'm all ears."

"We can't, but you can. One way is you have to stop dreaming and with my help, enter into all the worlds you created and kill your copy. In this case, yourself."

He moved on as he read my mind. That way would take forever, and in the end, how could I kill someone I entered without dying myself?

"The second option is to find your book."

I gave him a confused look. "What book?" How could a book help? We had bigger problems than something some book or religion could cure.

"This is not an ordinary book, this is *the* book, your book." Kreios lowered his voice as if he were scared someone might overhear us. "In the Bible, it talks of the Book of Life. In this book, the Creator writes the names of his children. If you die and your name is not found in this book, you will be cast into hell to burn forever."

I had listened to the story as a child in Sunday school. The saved people or the ones who trusted in Jesus Christ to save them would be written in this book. "I know the story."

"Well—" He hesitated, "you're not like others, not like other humans." The way he looked at me made me concerned. What did he mean, "not like other humans"?

"Mark, you are half human. No human can see his own Book of Life or even get to it. The Creator has it locked away in a room guarded by a powerful beasts that, if seen, this world would melt to even look upon their flesh. But your book is not among the ones locked away. It is on the earth somewhere, loose and hidden away, or stolen. We can rest assured that it is still here because you are still alive."

KIRK WALKED ACROSS THE street and made his way through the chaos surrounding the Merc building. Something was going on beyond the scope of the blackouts. He had a feeling they were in for a rough ride.

The parking garage was deserted, for the most part. Kirk found the elevator and punched in the code. He knew that in the science room there had to be some sort of device that could open this box. He would strap C4 to the side if he had to, but one way or another, he would get it open.

The door opened and the silence of the place made Kirk nervous. Lights were on down here and the elevator even worked. That was one thing the WJA had going for them—they were prepared for just about anything.

Something moved in the corner of Kirk's eye. He flinched and whipped around with his gun drawn. The box hit the floor and made a loud *thunk* sound. Standing in the hallway was a large man, black and huge, looking like a gorilla in the doorway was dwarfed by Big B's size.

"B! You scared the—what are you doing?" Kirk holstered his gun and walked toward the big man.

"Stay back! I'm infected…" He coughed and hunched over, holding onto the doorframe for support. "I got the virus. I was down here looking for any survivors." Big B rubbed a large hand across his forehead and coughed again.

"You're okay, I'm somehow immune. Isis is in the hospital, but I think I might have found the antidote." Kirk walked slowly toward B, and as he drew near, he saw large boils covering his arms and face. He had wet perspiration standing on his brow, and his t-shirt was soaked.

"B, you should be in bed, what are you doing to yourself?" Kirk helped him into a room and found a chair, and Big B collapsed into it with a grunt.

"I'm dead anyway, what does it matter? I thought I could help and at least save some…"

"Ah, we looked all over for you, where were you? Where is the rest of the group?"

"Don't know, I went home and fell sick, and once I saw the news, I came back here. Everyone was gone. I tried to call, but all the phones are down. This blackout has everything down—no phones, no power."

Kirk sat down in a chair across from Big B and rubbed his head. "Did you find anything?"

Big B shook his head. "Nothing I could use. You said you might have found an antidote?" His voice rose in anticipation.

"I think so, but it is in some sort of air-tight cooler. The thing is like a safe." Kirk got up and left the room. He retrieved the box and placed it on the desk in front of Big B. "See, here is the keypad, and feel how cold it is. It's like it has its own internal power source."

Big B looked at the box and turned it over and around, lifting it like it weighed no more than a lunch box. "No clue on the code?"

"No, but I found it in Taras Karjanski's condo." Big B smirked and coughed, and this time, blood came up. He spit out of the side of his mouth and wiped his lips.

"Man, this is the pits."

"Come on, man, you need to rest. Can I get you anything?" Kirk couldn't watch this guy die in front of him. He looked around the small office, saw a refrigerator and got up and opened it, finding soda and bottled water. He grabbed a can of Dr Pepper and a water. "Here, drink this."

"Thanks."

Big B opened the plastic top and downed the contents in three, big gulps. He sighed with relief and went back to examining the box. "I think I know how we can open it. In the lab, we have a scanner. It should be able to see fingerprints. If so, we can deduct from the prints what keys were used and start from there."

Kirk groaned and said. "I was hoping for a big Jaws of Life kind of thing and just tear the thing apart."

Big B smiled. "Nah, we can try that later. I don't want to damage what is inside if we don't have to."

"Too late for that, I dropped it, like, three times already. I figured if the thing wasn't rattling around, it's either empty, or the thing inside is protected somehow."

"Let's hope for the latter..."

Kirk nodded, reached over, and took the box. He muttered under his breath and promised himself that if he made it out alive, he was going to begin to work out more. The stupid thing weighed a ton.

Big B pushed himself to his feet and shuffled after Kirk. Kirk let him pass and followed him to the lab. The floor was empty, and the white lights gave the room a clean feel. Kirk blinked under the brightness of the bulbs. Big B looked even worse in this light.

"Set it down over there." Big B pointed to a long counter top with a plastic case sitting on top. The case was five feet tall, and square. A door on the end could be opened up to allow the user to insert whatever they wanted tested. Kirk set the box down and sighed.

"Now what?" Kirk asked.

Big B sat down hard in a rolling chair and said, "We hope and pray."

CHAPTER FOURTEEN

"WE HAVE TO GO back," Kreios moved toward me and I pulled back.

"No! I just got here, we can't leave." The thought of leaving Maria upstairs and having her wake up with… with someone else. I knew it would be me, but not the me that I was.

"If you stay much longer, real time will start and you have some business to take care of, or you could leave the key world in ruin." Kreios lowered his eyebrows and held out his hand.

"I thought you said that if I stayed here, this would become the key world."

"Yes, in time but not before the real key world topples and filters down to the rest of your little creations." A hint of anger laced his voice. It wasn't like I could control this thing. What did he want from me?

"I want you to go home, to stop this virus, and—"

Kreios mashed his lips together and stopped speaking.

"What? And what, Kreios?"

He looked down at the floor and said nothing. "We must go."

I sighed and nodded. "Fine." I took his hand, and a flash of bright light filled my skull. I felt like I was thrown from a speeding train.

Minutes, days, or even years could have passed in the in-between portal we traveled through. I couldn't tell, yet somehow I felt like some of my soul and life was being sucked away. This was not right, not supposed to even be possible.

I opened my eyes, and we were standing out in front of the Merc building. The CDC and the NYPD had the place locked down, and the sounds of reporters all talking at once made a hum cover the place.

My head spun, and I held onto Kreios's arm to steady myself. "Whoa... feels weird."

"Yes."

So full of wisdom, thanks for the insightful answer, Kreios. Then I remembered his mind reading abilities and cleared my throat. "Okay, what do I need to do? Didn't you have something else you were looking for?"

"I have recovered my property. There is no need to concern yourself with me. What do you know of this virus?" He walked away from the building and started down the sidewalk.

Virus? My head was still working on the half-human thing and all I wanted to do was find out what was going on with me and— "Virus? I'm sorry but that is not on my mind right now. I can always leave this reality and stop time for a while. I have to find a way to fix this mess I created… how can we do that without having me go back and kill all the versions of myself?"

Kreios seemed annoyed. "Outside of never dreaming again there is not much you can do. Killing the others would take time, but in the real world this wouldn't take that long in real time."

"You mean I have to really go around and try to nab a look at myself and kill them all off?" There had to be another way, some other plan that did not involve killing. I killed for a living, but this was different.

"There is one way…" Kreios stopped walking and leaned against a newsstand.

"That would be?"

"Find your book and write the ability away."

My jaw loosened and I could feel my brain working overtime to figure out what he was saying. "You mean I can write in my own book?"

Kreios nodded. That is why it is so important to find it. You can write in it, but others can, as well. If they write, erase, or tear a page from the book, it could tear this universe apart. That is why all the human books are under lock and key."

"Wait… you're telling me that my book is out there somewhere and some kid could tear a page from it and the part they took out would disappear—poof—gone as if it never existed?"

"Not as if it never existed, but it would never exist as in it will change the past and the future. With your powers and your book on the loose, there is the slim possibility that someone is out there writing in your book, unaware that it is changing your life."

I thought on this for a full minute. The time that passed seemed so pretend, as if a small hole opened up in the divide between me and some other reality. "So, my abilities may be because someone out there is messing with my book?"

"It is slim—almost impossible."

"Almost?"

"There are no guarantees. However, you are real and your abilities are real, and writing in the book is forbidden, so if someone were doing it, the host of heaven would know and put a stop to it at once. Nevertheless, we need to find that book before some *kid,* as you say, does tear out a page."

"This is crazy!" My head hurt, my teeth hurt, and my gut felt as if I just eaten five hot dogs all covered with onions. "Books and powers and other worlds, I don't know... I mean—"

Kreios slapped me with the back of his hand and a fire shot through my sore teeth and ran back to the base of my neck. "You are a man, now act like it, and do what you must to fix this problem. I do not care if you believe. The truth is the truth whether you believe in it or not. I do not have time to convince you anymore. We will find this book, you will fix this, and I will be on my way. Or I shall kill you and kill every one of your other selves and be done with the whole mess."

I rubbed my face and nodded. "Sorry, I was—" My pride hurt at knowing that Kreios could have just killed me and never even talked to me in the first place. I was grateful to be alive.

"I have a plan to keep anyone from writing in your book, but it requires you to trust me."

"Yes… yes, I'll do whatever it requires." Kreios let a half smile cross his face.

"We have to go back to the beginning and lock your book. If you write a code or a password into the soul of the book so that only the person with the password can write in it, that may be just what we need to buy us some time."

I nodded. "Okay, what do we have to do?"

Kreios held out his hand. "Take my hand."

———∞———

THE LARGE PLASTIC BOX filled with a light green fog and covered the metal cooler. Kirk stood with his arms crossed and glared at the green fog with a look of disdain. He was beginning to wonder if their hopes were in vain, or if this was the answer.

"The gas has an element in it that will stick to any kind of oil, and we have tested and perfected this compound so it will stick to the oil on the skin. Anywhere someone has touched it will show up in green after it is done." Big B was sitting in a chair and Kirk could tell that he was not feeling well. His skin was more pale then normal and he coughed every few minutes. The sound made Kirk shiver.

The green fog began to thin out, and in a matter of minutes, it was gone altogether. Kirk looked toward Big B and got the nod. Opening up the case, he reached inside, and taking the box by the corners, he slid it out and turned it so the keypad faced them.

The numbered keypad had bright green smudges on

five numbers. two, four, five, six, and eight.

Kirk looked at Big B and said, "Okay, we got the numbers, but what order are they in?"

Big B pushed with his feet, and his chair rolled toward the counter top. He began typing on a keyboard, and the flat screen monitor in front of him came to life. "We should be able to run the numbers and get the possible combinations. There will be a lot of them... This could take weeks to figure out."

"We don't have weeks, we have hours. Look at you, B. You will be dead in a few days if you don't get the antidote." Kirk's voice raised and he paced the floor rubbing his stubbly head.

Big B coughed and doubled over. He spit out some blood and wiped his mouth. "I know... I don't know what else we can do..."

Kirk went over to the box and punched in the numbers two-four-five-six-eight. A red light flashed and read, "access denied." He cursed and looked again at the keypad. The sound of Big B typing over his shoulder made him feel the sheer impossibility of the number possibilities.

He noticed that the number five had more smudges then the rest of the numbers and wondered if it was because it was used twice. Kirk punched in two-four-six-eight-five, and five again. A green light flashed, the door gears hummed, and the door slid forward a few inches. Kirk's heart leapt.

"I think I got it!" Kirk said. Big B rolled over and watched as the door hinged down and lay flat. The opening beyond had ice on all six sides of the box. Steam came from the box, and inside was a metal container. Kirk reached in, took the round cylinder out, and noticed that there were three total.

He handed the first one to Big B and took another one. The cylinders were stainless steel and the size of a hairspray canister. They had screw-top lids and were held in place with thin metal holders that suspended them in the middle of the cooler. That explained why they didn't rattle around.

Kirk held his breath, unscrewed the lid, and prayed that this was the antidote. The cold container held a full syringe with a red liquid. Kirk let out a breath and looked toward Big B. He had his open, as well, and held the syringe up for Kirk to see.

"How do we know if it is the antidote and not another virus?" Kirk asked. He never thought they would really find it so fast, and now that they had it, he was wondering if it was the real deal or just another, more violent virus.

Big B looked at Kirk, down at the syringe in his hand, and said. "Only one way to find out." He pulled off the protective cover, took the exposed needle, stuck it into his arm, and pushed the plunger down. Before Kirk could protest, the red contents disappeared into his arm.

He gritted his teeth and a faraway look crossed his face. "You okay?"

"It is so cold... I can feel it running through my veins. Weird... I feel the same, but it will take time to work. You have that one for Isis and the third we can give to the CDC so they can produce more for the rest of the infected."

Kirk placed the empty syringe back into the container, took the other one, and stopped dead in his tracks. He remembered the power failure and the other coolers full of more of the deadly virus, and looked down at the two cylinders in his hands.

"We have a big problem. I was so focused on saving Isis, I didn't think of the impact of Taras's little love nest." Big B looked at him and lowered his eyebrows.

"What are you talking about?"

Kirk turned and sighed. "I found this box in his command center in the building where he lived. There are three walk-in coolers, more like freezers, and two of them held container after container of what looked like more of the virus. The labels were from other countries, and when the power went out, the coolers shut down. It's only a matter of time before they thaw out."

"So…"

"Mark said that the virus activates at room temperature. If it stays frozen, the virus is harmless, but if that cooler thaws out, it will take out New York and quite possibly the rest of the country."

CHAPTER FIFTEEN

THE AIR TURNED FROM a city smell of hot asphalt and urine to a deep cleansing scent of pine trees and fresh spring water. Kreios stood next to me. Without a sound, he pulled me to the ground behind a clump of big green ferns.

"What—?"

Kreios shushed me with his hand over my mouth. I looked at him and he whispered in a low hushed voice. "I must not be seen. You have to do this on your own. In a few moments, I will come around the corner with a book, and you must convince me to give it to you. When you have it, bring it back to me, and I will show you how to protect it."

I nodded even though what he just said made no sense. He would come around the corner? I turned to ask a question, but Kreios was gone.

Great. Just what I needed. I was alone in the woods, in some other world and possibly some other time. I pulled a fern away from my eyes and looked out through tall, pine trees and down into the long valley below.

The night air smelled sweet and the full moon hung low in the sky, casting an almost day-like light across the woods in long streams through the trees. Shadows moved in ways I'd not seen since I was a kid hunting with my dad. It reminded me of simpler times, and in some ways, a past that was just an illusion.

I could hear the soft babble of a stream in the distance, and to my surprise, something else moved to my left. It was so slight that I almost mistook it for the natural sounds of the forest. I saw a creature move not ten feet from me, and I held my breath. I saw Kreios, or maybe his twin, hunch down behind some thick bushes. His back was to me. He was wearing a long robe, and he held something in his hands.

A book.

The sword that hung at his waist stopped me from standing up and calling out to him. It wasn't the same Kreios I came here with, or if it was, he did a quick clothes change.

Beyond Kreios-number-two, I could hear another sound. This one was loud and sounded like two people not trained in keeping quiet in the woods; they tromped through underbrush and were talking loudly. They moved, hacking at bushes and grunting in some other language. The men never came into view, but turned in another direction and soon faded.

Kreios stood motionless, and as soon as the danger was gone, he moved and started up the small hill toward me. I didn't want to startle him, so I stood up and held my hands out, palms up, in a submissive gesture.

"Hello," I said in a calm voice.

Kreios stopped and his sword was out in an amazing show of speed. He stood still, so I took a step toward him and repeated my greeting. He gave me a curious look and looked me up and down, most likely noticing my clothes. I held out my hands wider and took another step toward him.

"My name is Mark—Mark Appleton. I need to speak with you." Kreios did not seem to fear me, and when he spoke, my heart sank. It was in some other language, one I did not understand.

In my training, I was programmed with many languages, but nothing he said seemed to ring a bell. It had a faint Hebrew tone to it, so I decided to try some Hebrew. I repeated my introduction in Hebrew and his eyes grew large. He responded in the same tongue, but his language was more formal then I was used to.

"I am Kreios in your human tongue. My true name is not one any human can speak, for it is not of this world." His voice was the same, and the feeling that I knew him in the future made this whole interaction seem unreal.

"I am not here to fight. I just want to talk." I let my hands fall to my sides and stepped closer as he replaced his sword in its sheath.

"I know that you do not know me, that I am dressed in strange clothing. But I am not here to harm you—in fact, I need your help."

Kreios eyed me and looked over his shoulder. After hearing nothing, I must have satisfied his curiosity, and he pointed to a large rock formation just to my right. "We can talk over there, I am being pursued by the Brotherhood, and it would do me no good to have to fight them with you here. I do not see a sword, and without defense, you will only slow me down."

I nodded, and we walked toward the rock formation. He stayed just out of reach behind me. I moved ahead and found a small hidden area on the backside. I sat down on the ground and waited.

Kreios took a seat across from me and looked at me as if I were the strangest thing he had ever seen. I started things off. I explained where I was from, and he listened without so much as a raised eyebrow. "I know this may be hard to believe, but I promise you that I am telling you the truth." I left out the part about how his future self was the one who helped me get here.

Kreios breathed in a sigh and said. "I believe you. As I said, I am not of this world, and time is a thin and unstable thing. You say you are here to talk to me, that I can help you and your world in some way."

"Yes, we have a problem, and I am part of the problem… I mean, I am most of the problem. I am told that I have a book, one that, in the wrong hands, could ruin my life and somehow—my world."

Kreios looked down at the book in his hands and then back up at me. "You said your name was Mark? Is that your birth name, or was it something different?"

"I think it was always Mark, but I was adopted… I have kind of a mixed up past."

Kreios touched the skin of the book's cover, and with gentle hands, he opened it and stared at the page. "You and I are linked in some way." He paused. "This conversation is not just a part of your past, but your future as well."

I didn't know what he was saying. How did he know what my past was or how this could change the future? "I don't understand."

"I know. Look at the page, and never read anything more than the page I am going to show you." Kreios handed me the book, and I looked down at the page. It was made of some sort of thin skin or paper. I wondered if paper was even invented at this time, but somehow I thought that this book could be anything, no matter what time it was in.

My eyes took in the letters written in a scrawling handwriting. The words and the handwriting looked familiar. Almost as if—it was my own. The words I read made me draw in a breath.

"And Mark said, "I don't understand."

Kreios said. "I know. Look at the page, and never read anything more than the page I am going to show you." Kreios handed the book to Mark, and he looked down at the page...

The words stopped, and I stared at the page trying to comprehend what I was seeing. "What is going on?"

Mark said. "What is going on?"

The words appeared as I spoke them, the ink dying the page. The realization hit me and my head swam. I was holding *my* book. The book of life that no human could ever see, the one that only someone not of this world could have access to, and here I was holding it in my lap.

MOOCH LEFT HIS LITTLE hideout, took his newly acquired cab, and drove into the city on back roads. He managed to get past the Army that now was set up on every major street and road leading into the city.

The president had ordered everyone to stay inside, and he enacted martial law. The country had no power, and what the United States didn't know was that it was not just the country, but the world.

Mooch was pleased with himself, and the passenger in his mind stood up and told him how wonderful he was. Why had he gone on so long not doing what he wanted? Why had he tried to do the right thing when doing bad felt so good?

Mooch was wearing a camo uniform, and he gave himself the rank of major, so if anyone came across him, he could move in and out of the city without much interference. He parked the cab in the back of the hospital, walked around to the front, flashed identification, and the CDC guy at the door let him in after he suited up.

The generators at the hospital were now running, but that wouldn't last. No, Mooch had big plans for this little place of refuge. He wanted to see someone, an old friend's girlfriend. "Isis, you are going to suffer for your choice in men. I am sorry to tell you, but Kirk Weston is just plain bad luck. Bad luck all around."

The main floor of the hospital was a mass of chaos. Nurses and doctors were running in and out of rooms, trying to keep everyone calm, and helping the sick. It was the same on all the floors throughout the building.

After 9/11, people were easy to scare. Terrorists and the thought of them striking again, mixed with the attack

Taras Karjanski unleashed, made the people highly sensitive. The blackout and the stock market crash did exactly what they were intended to do: strike fear into the minds of the people. If the people lived in fear, they could be controlled.

No outside communication, no contact with the rest of the world, no internet, or Google, no information to reveal what was going on—just the voices in everyone's minds, just the fears rising up. Once they were let out to run free, they would destroy and kill in order to protect themselves.

Mooch took the stairs, not fearing the virus. He did not think he would contract the disease, or if he did, he believed he would be immune. The power he felt running through his veins was intoxicating. He felt unstoppable, he felt like what he thought God must feel like.

As he climbed, he noticed that he wasn't even breathing hard. He was not only strong in mind, but in body as well. Once he found the correct floor, he walked down the hall and looked into each room until he found the room he wanted. He smiled and almost laughed aloud. He felt so good, and the things he had to look forward to made him want to giggle like a little schoolgirl.

CHAPTER SIXTEEN

GRAY FEATHERS FLUFFED IN a slight breeze as a fat pigeon sat looking out over Main Street in downtown Los Angles. It twisted its head so fast that it appeared impossible to stay attached to the pigeon. It looked like it would snap off. However, the plump pigeon didn't seem to mind the quick movement.

Parked below, a yellow cab stood at the curb, and a military truck moved down the middle of the street at just under four miles per hour. This was the first stage, fear. People stayed inside, and the power would come back on for ten minutes every day, but the backup systems soon overloaded, and the city shut off once again.

Gas credits did not go out because the only ones that could buy the expensive fuel were government officials and military. Tonight, the pigeon and his friends would watch as the next stage took over.

Anger and panic.

Looters would run the streets, and the military force would not be able to stave off this mob like they did before. The small pockets of rioters were the misfits who looked for an opportunity to steal and take advantage of any situation. This new mob would be the stockbrokers and soccer moms who were driven by the fear that the food would be gone before the country could recover from the crises.

Taking flight, the pigeon dropped to the street and found some garbage to snack on. A muttering sound behind it made the bird turn its head in a lightning quick twist. A man stood looking at the bird with crazy, bloodshot eyes. He held onto a pistol. His white shirt was torn and dirty, and his black tie hung loose around his neck.

The pigeon took three steps back, and the man looked past the bird and out to the street. A second military vehicle moved down the street at a slow pace, looking up and down the side streets.

The man cursed, raised his gun, and fired. The sound startled the bird, and he took flight with his little heart pounding in his chest. A rapid succession of gunfire sounded, and a scream.

The pigeon looked back and saw the man with the gun lying on his back, blood pooling around his motionless body. A soldier stepped from the vehicle and checked the man on the ground. He shook his head, got back into the vehicle, and continued down the street.

———⧯———

"MAYBE WE CAN CALL the FBI or the CDC and tell

them about the coolers." Kirk said as he flipped open his cell. He put the phone to his ear, his eyes flashed irritation, and he turned the phone over and smacked it two times.

"It's dead…"

Big B stood up and grunted in pain. "Battery?"

"No, got no signal. Says there's no service."

Big B lowered his heavy eyebrows and picked up a phone that sat a few feet away. It was on a land-line. He smiled. "Cell towers must be out, but we still got land-lines." He dialed 911 but got a busy signal.

"Great, busy."

"We can let the boys upstairs know on our way out. We need to get them this antidote anyway. Hopefully, they can reproduce it in time," Kirk said.

Kirk shoved one of the canisters into his pocket and held the other one in his hand. Big B looked at the bulge in his pocket and shook his head. "They will see that a mile away. Give it here, I can put it in mine."

Kirk took it out and handed it to Big B. B took the canister and put in into a large pocket in his cargo pants. It looked like nothing was there unless they patted them down. Kirk figured they would be able to sneak them out.

Kirk looked at his watch. "How long do you think we have until that freezer cools down to room temp.?"

"Depends on how cold it was to start with. But I figure, as long as the door stays closed, we got 24 hours, maybe longer. But best not to push our luck." Big B glanced at Kirk. "Why do you ask?"

Kirk sighed. "I have this feeling that, if we take the antidote to the CDC, we will be tied up for hours, maybe longer, and Isis is real sick. I want to take this to her and help her first. Thought if we have time, well…"

Big B opened the door leading into the hallway and turned back to stare at Kirk. He patted the lump in his pocket and nodded. "You might be right; they will want a full report on how we found it and all the details. Could take days to get free of them. Okay, we take this to Isis, and once we know that she will make it, we go to the CDC. In the meantime, we need to get some sort of message to them that there are two freezers in the Grove, and that they contain more of the virus."

Kirk nodded with relief. Isis filled his mind with every waking thought. All he could think about was her and how she could be dead right now. They could still be too late.

They took the elevator up to the parking garage. Kirk was glad the backup generators were still working. They made sure to turn off all the lights and lock down the center before they left, just in case someone found the underground facility.

Yellow crime tape and red warning tape crisscrossed the doors and were strung across just about every post and pillar on the outside of the building. Most of the CDC vans and police cars were gone. All the people who were still alive must have been transported to a hospital or a different location. The building was sealed off, and a guard was placed at every entrance.

Kirk followed Big B down the ramp. They looked over the side and saw the rent-a-cops walking a pattern from one side of the building to the other. Kirk shuddered at the thought of what his future might be. He could very well end up doing this same kind of dead-end job, reliving the past, and regretting all his bad decisions.

"Look at that!" Big B said in a hushed whisper. Kirk followed his pointing finger and gasped. The streets of New York were deserted. The sun was beginning to set, and a warm glow flooded the streets and cast an orange hue on all the buildings and parked cars. The hum that was the city was all but silent. Kirk never really took notice of the way the city seemed to breathe, to be a living thing, until now. It felt dead.

"No way…" Kirk couldn't believe what he was seeing. It was like something out of a science fiction, end-of-all-days movie. Cars were parked in the middle of the street, hot dog vendor carts were abandoned, and the only cars on the road were military vehicles. In the distance, a siren blared, and thick, black smoke billowed up a few streets over.

"How long were we down there?" Big B rubbed his eyes as if clearing them would change what they were looking at.

"Not that long, not long enough to turn the world into this."

Roadblocks were set up, and the empty buildings and sidewalks gave Kirk a sinking feeling. This couldn't be happening… just a day ago, the city was busy beehive of activity. People walked in packed groups and talked on phones and drank fancy coffee.

Big B and Kirk were frozen in place, not comprehending—or not wanting to understand what was happening.

A loud speaker on a portable pole squawked a message played from a recording.

"For your own safety, stay indoors. There is a strict

curfew. No one is to be outdoors after 8 p.m. Do not
go out after dark, and do not try to use electricity. This
curfew is for your own safety."

A movement caught Kirk's attention, and he turned to look up the street. Big B did the same, and as the sun hid behind the massive buildings that made New York what it was, a glow bounced and bobbed, moving, muttering.

A mob of people came from doorways and held flashlights and torches. Broken chair legs wrapped in rags and lit up gave the mob a Middle Ages feel. "Time to go." Big B moved down the ramp as the sound of approaching vehicles roared down the empty street. That would be the Army, or the National Guard.

Kirk hurried after Big B, and they ducked into the alley and ran two blocks with the ring of gunfire to their backs. Kirk cursed and wondered why the people were rioting. Food, fuel, fear? Maybe all three.

Kirk stopped just before they entered a main street. He looked around the corner and didn't see anyone, but just as they stepped from the shadow of the alley, a shout rang out.

"Hey, you! Stop!" Kirk and Big B glanced at each other and ran across the street and into the alley on the other side. Shouts and angry voices followed them, and the smack of boots on pavement made Kirk pick up the pace.

"Stop, or I'll shoot!" The order came from a different voice. Kirk dove behind a large blue dumpster and pulled his .45 free. Big B was across the way, hiding behind a crate.

The boots stopped, and the click of buckles against

metal was the only sound. "Come on, come out, and we won't shoot. We just want to talk." They didn't sound military. But they didn't sound like white-collar bankers either.

Kirk waited and willed his heart to calm down. He swore that it could be heard by their little friends. Leaning down as quietly as he could, Kirk looked under the dumpster and saw black combat boots not three feet away. Two sets, one for each of them.

Kirk held up two fingers and Big B nodded. Big B had a gun in his hand. Kirk didn't have time to wonder where he got it or how he carried it without him noticing. Kirk held up three fingers and counted down.

Three.

Two.

One.

CHAPTER SEVENTEEN

KREIOS STAYED UNDER COVER and watched the exchange between Mark and himself. He could not hear what they were saying, and he dared not open up his mind to read Mark's thoughts for fear that he would hear himself and something terrible would happen.

It took years of training to learn to close off his mind, and not only that but shut it down to the point that he was invisible to anyone who might have the mind reading ability. Most who could do it could sense the person even if they could not read thoughts. Kreios could wall off his thoughts and keep from detection, but he had to concentrate.

Mark took the book from Kreios and looked down at the page. His body tensed and as Kreios watched. He knew that this was the right book. They exchanged a few words, and Mark stood up and held out his hand. The two shook hands, and Mark walked off heading to the last spot he and Kreios had parted ways.

Kreios looked at himself and wondered what he was going to do. The strange part was the new memory of the meeting with Mark and how he now did know what he was thinking.

He knew that this book was now in the hands of its owner, and he wondered if Mark really knew who he was. He doubted it; the poor man seemed to be confused and not sure what he was doing.

Kreios moved from his hiding spot and slowly and silently made his way toward where Mark would be waiting. He looked back and saw that his other self was sitting down, had pulled out a pipe, and began to pack it with tobacco. That was one thing he missed, that pipe. In this age, smoking was looked down upon, so he trained himself not to do it, but it took some doing.

Mark stood looking around, and when he saw Kreios, a smile spread across his face. "Got it." He held up the book, and Kreios nodded.

"Good, now let's see if this will work."

———⚭———

I HELD ONTO THE book and felt the warmth it produced. Not only was it warm, but it felt as if it were alive somehow. I was still in shock as to this book's existence and to the power it held. I always knew something like this had to be real, but to see it with my own eyes, to hold it and read the words just as they were written, was something different.

I had to find out what was going on. I knew now that I was mixed up in something more than just a secret group that fought injustice. I was more than a crime-fighting assassin. This was something supernatural.

Kreios said that people, humans—that was the word he used—humans could not see their books, that they was under lock and key. However, non-humans could... things that were not all human could see their books, and others could steal them and use them as a weapon against their owners.

"So now what?" I handed the book to Kreios. He took it and touched the cover with gentle fingers, as if the book were made of glass and could be broken.

"*We* do nothing. You will do what we need in order to protect your book. You cannot keep it or take it with you through time so we must entrust it to me and hope I do not fail in protecting it from the Brotherhood."

"Who is this 'Brotherhood' you keep talking about? Are they the ones who were chasing that... er... you?"

Kreios nodded. "Yes, they are demonic powers that are on the earth to eradicate our kind. Their only mission is to kill all of us, and once they are done, we will be no more." Kreios handed me the book back and said, "We do not have much time here. It is dangerous, and we can talk of these things another time."

I flashed him a frown, but even from the short time that I had known this man, I knew that it would be pointless to argue with him. The man had no sense of humor and took everything so seriously.

"Okay, tell me what to do so we can get out of here. This time travel thing is not for me. Too much can go wrong."

"Open the book to the first page,"

"But you said not to read any of it… I mean not you, but the other you."

"Kreios nodded. " As long as you do not read into the future, you will be fine. The danger is that, by reading the book, you will see things you might want to change. This, for most, is a temptation that is too strong to resist."

"How can I read into the future? I saw how it worked—it was writing as things happened, so everything I do or think is written down, but nothing was on the page before."

"This is true. The book is a real-time record of the owner's life and thoughts. Yet some things are set in time and space, some things we cannot change and are a part of our future no matter what we do. These things are written by the Creator and cannot be altered. These are the words you must not read."

I pondered his words for a minute. I was under the impression that I had free will. Wasn't that something all humans had—a free will to choose their own path, their own future?

Kreios answered my thoughts. That was getting annoying.

"Yes, every human has a free will. You are not all human, so some of the rules do not apply to you."

"Again with the '*not all human*'! What am I then? You keep alluding to my lack of humanity, so what am I? Alien? Demon? Half ape?" I was getting angry, but at the same time, I knew that this was not the time or the place to be having this conversation. We had a limited time, and I knew that every minute here was one more minute we were in danger of being discovered or killed.

"Never mind. Forget I said anything!" I sat down and placed the book in my lap. "What do I do?"

Kreios sat next to me and said, "Open it to the first page."

I opened the book and saw my name written at the top in some strange language, yet I understood it. I saw it, and knew it was not English, but could still read it.

"Now, all you have to do is write in the book, and whatever you write will happen." Kreios looked down at the page with a calm expression on his face.

I patted my pockets and found a sharpie attached to my keychain. It was one of those little ones. I never used it but it was something K gave me, and I kept it there just in case. I guess this was a "just in case."

"Is this okay?" I held up the mini sharpie. Kreios nodded. "Good, because that's all I got. Now, what do I write?"

Kreios thought a minute. "Write the exact words I tell you. Do not alter it in any way. Do you understand?"

"Yes."

I took the cap off and waited.

"At the top of the page, write this under your name: *This book is to be protected and secured from all unauthorized alterations. The owner of the book is to be the only one with the ability to tamper or alter in any way the contents of this book. Any and all writing is to be stricken and rendered useless unless authorized by the owner. This decree is irreversible even by the owner of this book.*"

Kreios rubbed his chin and nodded. "That should do. That way no one can force you to reverse this rule.

Although you can still be forced to write in the book if someone were to capture you."

"I'm not worried about that. I just don't want anyone to use it without my knowing it. That could get ugly in a hurry."

"Now, take it back to me, and tell me to protect it at all costs or put it in a safe place."

"Not that it will do any good. You don't have it now and don't know where it is, so what good will it do?"

Kreios sighed… "Because I remember you telling me these words. I know it will do no good, but you still tell me."

"Ah." This was weird, way too weird—even for me.

I closed the book and stood up. "Okay, I'll be right back."

Kreios didn't say anything, and he stood up fast, he still didn't make a sound. I was amazed by how light on his feet he was. This was not over; I had to know what was going on even if it meant I took the information by force. As soon as we got back, I was going to have a talk with Kreios.

CHAPTER EIGHTEEN

THE CLIP OF A heel hitting the pavement sounded at the exact moment Kirk and Big B sprang from their temporary hiding places. The two men held small submachine guns low at their hips, telling Kirk in an instant that these men knew how to hold them and thus knew how to use them.

This fact was not relevant, but it still made killing the two men feel better. Kirk didn't want to kill an innocent civilian who just wanted to protect his family. These men were hired guns, probably some militia group that, up until now was working underground, but with the crisis, they decided this was a good time to run wild.

The first shot was not from Kirk, and later, Kirk would look at this as a failure on his part. He prided himself in his skill in battle, his wit, and quick reactions. To have a big, slow black man beat him on the draw (not to mention that B was sick and not feeling his best) just made matters worse. But, the job got done, so in the end it was just his feelings that were hurt, or pride, whichever—

Kirk loved the way, in situations like this, the world seemed to slow down, as if everything were in slow motion. He saw a small red dot form on the forehead of the man to Kirk's right. The back of his skull exploded like a watermelon as his finger squeezed down on the trigger and a flash of fire escaped the muzzle of his weapon.

Bullets sprayed outward and up in an arching blaze of orange light as the man fell backward. Kirk saw all this, and at the same time, double tapped the man to the left just as he was trained. Never one shot, always two. You might miss and the second was to seal the deal. Big B, on the other hand, was not a cop; he was a trained assassin and didn't fear a miss.

Kirk didn't miss either. He took the safe shot one inch high but still through the heart. The advancing man wore black cargo pants, a black twill sweater, and a black ball cap. He staggered to a stop and sank to his knees. His eyes were wide in shock, and Kirk looked past him toward the street to see if more were on the way.

The empty streets echoed with footfalls. Kirk snatched up the submachine gun, and Big B did the same. They might need these later, but for now they had to get out of this alley.

"Three more coming…" Big B said in a gasping voice.

"How do you know?"

"Counted their steps. Three… one is lighter, maybe a kid or a woman."

Kirk didn't ask. He took off down the alley, and Big B followed. They came to the corner and made a left. It was a side alley, and trashcans were tipped over, laundry hung above on lines of twine, and a few rats scurried when they rounded the corner.

A scream of anger sounded behind them and a shot rang out. The brick just behind Kirk shattered just as he left the line of sight of the three attackers.

More footfall and yells.

Kirk picked up the pace, and Big B seemed to be keeping up. The alley ended, and a chain link fence blocked the way. Kirk started to climb when Big B grabbed his shirt collar.

"We can't outrun them. We need to hide, make them think we ran."

Kirk grunted and cursed. "Where?"

Big B looked around and motioned toward an archway and a large wooden door. It was partially blocked by trash and some electric transformer looking thing. The door did not look like it had been used in some time. Kirk and Big B ran to it and hunched down. The sound of breathing was all Kirk could hear.

Kirk leaned against Big B and felt the heat coming from the big man's body. His breath was hot on his neck as they waited. They didn't have to wait long.

Not fifty seconds after they hid, the three attackers rounded the corner at a dead run. The first to come into view was a tall man wearing the same black-on-black gear and holding the same brand of submachine gun.

Then a stockier man and a woman came, all dressed the same and huffing from running or anger, Kirk didn't know which.

The tall man took hold of the chain link fence and

began to climb. Big B made a hand gesture to let them go. Kirk figured he didn't want to shoot a woman, and if they ran off they could escape some other way.

Kirk nodded but didn't share the same feelings. He had to restrain himself from mowing them all down even if it was in the back. They had tried to kill them, and if he died, that meant Isis would die, and he would not let that happen. He saw the three climb the fence and after some doing, they made it over.

Kirk was a little disappointed that they got away, but he figured this would not be the first time something like this would happen. The world was going to hell in a hurry, and this was just the beginning.

Kirk stood up and looked after the three black figures as they moved down the alley, turned onto the street, and disappeared. Kirk knew that the last thing he should have done was stand up and not make sure the alley was clear before he stood up. But it was too late now…

He heard the sound of metal clicking on metal, and he knew they had missed one. Filled with anger at himself for being so stupid, Kirk turned as fast as he could. A burst of gunfire echoed through the small alley and he felt pain in his shoulder.

Spinning as he fell, Kirk saw a boy not more than fourteen holding a snubnose machine gun at hip level. He did not smile, he did not blink; he just fired and watched Kirk fall.

Big B put two bullets in the boy's head, and at this range, the boy's head did not explode out the back but caved in on itself. The body fell to the pavement, and Kirk saw bright flashing lights and the sound of more angry screams back down the alley.

Blood leaked out around the boy and Kirk saw his shoe just before he blacked out. It was a Vans flat bottom shoe, white with tan trim. *He was just a kid... a kid.*

⎯⎯⎯⎯⎯∞∞⎯⎯⎯⎯⎯

ISIS SLEPT, AND HER breathing, even though labored, was soft and steady. Mooch watched her from a chair in the corner of the room. He studied the tubes running down her throat and the IV in her arm. Machines hummed and made beeping sounds, and her heartbeat made a jagged line jump up and down in a hypnotic rhythm on a screen to his right.

Mooch sat for over an hour and listened to the voice in his head.

"She is so beautiful. You deserve to have someone like that love you and take care of you. Kirk Weston should be alone, not you. Weston does not deserve her."

His need grew, and like a smoker giving in to have one more for old time's sake, Mooch could not resist the temptation. He thought about how it must feel to be loved, how he once felt when he was loved by Emily.

Emily—sweet Emily. She was the only one who understood him. And she was also the one who shot him, tried to kill him! No—no, it was Kirk's fault. She was trying to shoot Kirk, not him.

Isis groaned and turned her head from side to side as if plagued by a nightmare. He wondered what she dreamed about—if it was of killing, or if the people she had killed haunted her in her dreams.

Mooch could still feel the cab driver's struggling

hands reaching back to try to stop him. He still saw the imploring eyes of the woman as she died and the little light went out in her soul.

He felt sick at the thought, but not because what he did made him feel bad. It was the need, the urge to kill again. It was like a deep hunger—one that would not let up, not let him be.

"She will satisfy you. After her, you will never hunger again."

He could now feel the thing inside of his brain moving like a snake in and out of his thoughts. Mooch was not sure what thoughts were his anymore; they all seemed to run together in a tangle of voices. Was he even there anymore?

"We are one. You are me, and I am you. This is the way life was meant to be lived. No rules, no restrictions, and no one telling us what to do."

The lights flickered overhead and went out. The machines kept on running on battery power, but in an hour or so, they would fail as well. Mooch let a smile cross his face, and he stood up and leaned over Isis, breathing in the scent of her hair.

"I'm sorry. Kirk made me do this. He is the one responsible, not me. I'm sorry but *we* have to do this." Mooch whispered, and in the glow of the monitor his face turned red. His eyes burned with hate, and he resembled a devil. Raising his right arm high above his head, a shaft of darkness swirled around and became solid in the shape of a jagged, black sword.

Mooch felt the sword in his hand and the power that ran up his arm and into his brain. It was like a warm line of energy, and as it filtered through his body, he gnawed on his tongue and muttered something in an unknown language.

"Set her free. Let us set her free, my brother!"

———— ∞∞ ————

I STOOD ALONE IN the woods, breathing and watching the bloated moon. Kreios-number-two was gone with my book, and my heart sank with the realization that I was not in control of my own destiny. I liked to feel some control, to be on top of things, but it seemed that my life was spiraling out of control.

A bird chirped, and I could hear frogs belching by the babbling stream. The scent of pine needles and the mixture that was the forest made me smile. It was this quiet and beauty that reminded me of better times. I filled my lungs and sat down, not worried about if Kreios would find me. I suspected he was watching and giving me time to process.

I thought of Maria and my son, Samson. The name Samson, how it was another version of Sam, did not escape me. My world was similar to the one I had with Maria. *Did I name him Samson because I remembered Sam?* I remembered bits and pieces. Like most memories, they come with trigger points—a smell, sound, or moment. I remembered how, after K and Sam died, Maria and I fell in love and married. After we became pregnant, I wanted to keep the memory of K and Sam alive, so we decided to name him Samson.

I sat down on a flat rock and ran a hand through my hair. My head hurt, and I could feel a throbbing behind my eyes. This was not supposed to happen—couldn't happen. Reality was real; the dreams I had were just that—dreams. They couldn't overlap and become real.

"God, I know I have not prayed in a long time. I'm not what I should be, and I feel like I don't have any right to even talk to you. But I'm in trouble here. I'm so lost, so alone, and I don't know what to do."

I could feel my heart fill with fear and hope. Fear because I didn't know what to do and thought that I might make the wrong choice. Hope because somewhere in the back of my mind, I knew God was real, knew that he, if anyone, could help me, and I hoped he would.

I felt dumb, and hot tears welled up in my eyes. I let myself cry, and even though it was not a manly thing to do, I didn't care. This was beyond me, too much to take on by myself.

Tears ran down my cheeks, and I let them go unhindered. My chest heaved, and I sobbed, not knowing what I was supposed to do or even how to ask.

"Please help me! I can't do this. I'm willing to do whatever you want. I'm so sorry for doing it my way all the time. I know now that without your help, I am nothing." The events of the last few years all poured out of me as if a dam inside of me had broken open. Old feelings and hidden hurts filled with the images of things I had done consumed my mind.

I saw the men I killed in the cabin, the look of rage on their faces. Even justified, it still had an impact on me. I smelled the liquor and cigar smoke in the room of the Magician and saw the bullet as it ejected and pierced his skull. All the men I killed… their faces, their voices haunted me. I knew what I did to them was justified in my mind, but still, somewhere deep inside, I knew my soul was not meant to kill.

I wanted to save people, wanted to protect my family and my country. But at what cost? Was the cost my own soul, my heart, and my sanity? Was it worth it? I didn't know anymore. At one time I would have said yes, but now…

My body shook, and I could feel my face burn as I let all the years of pain and confusion out. This was the true Mark Appleton. The killer, the tightrope walker, the man without fear, and the one who was supposed to have it all together. Here I was in some other time, weeping like a child because I was alone.

K whispered in my ear, and Maria hugged me, but I didn't know if they were real. My life was just a sham, a fake reality, and nothing was real anymore.

I felt the presence of someone shadowing over me, and a strong arm enveloped me. Kreios took me in his arms and spoke in some other tongue. His voice was deep and soft, soothing, and after a while, I calmed down.

"This is you, Mark Appleton. You must release all your fears and doubt." Kreios turned and looked at me. It felt like he was looking into my very soul.

"You need to trust me. I can help you, but you must open up your mind and let what is real just happen even if it should be impossible. With God—with El—nothing is impossible."

I nodded and wiped my eyes with the back of my hand. The heavy burden that I was carrying for so long seemed to drop from my shoulders. I couldn't believe how good I felt, how free. I sucked in some more of the fresh mountain air and smiled. "Okay… okay. Let's go home."

CHAPTER NINETEEN

KIRK WESTON OPENED HIS eyes minutes after he passed out. Big B stood over him and was slapping his face. The sting brought Kirk back, and he wondered if the big guy was going to keep it up or stop now that he was awake.

"Okay... enough, I'm awake."

Kirk rubbed his aching head and blinked to clear his vision. As soon as he moved, his shoulder screamed out at him.

"It went clean through, you should be fine—here," Big B handed him a piece of torn cloth, and Kirk pressed it to the wound and grimaced. It hurt, and as he stood up, the world spun, but he managed to stay on his feet.

"Let's go, we gotta get out of here." Big B nodded and got under Kirks shoulder and began to half drag him toward the street. "I got it..." Kirk pushed away, stumbled, and almost fell again.

"You passed out, give it a minute."

"We don't have a minute..." Kirk focused on the ground in front of him and started walking. He felt the throbbing pain in his shoulder and used that pain to keep him alert. This was stupid, the world is going to hell, and looters are out shooting people.

Big B followed and stayed close to Kirk. Kirk could smell blood and sweat as the big man crowded him. He wondered if the he was hurt or if the blood smell was coming from him.

Moments later, voices came around the corner and three more people dressed in black started shooting at them. Kirk cursed and turned to face his death. Big B released his grip on Kirk, raised his stolen automatic machine gun, and laid down a wave of fire. Two of the men fell screaming, and Kirk fired but missed the third. He was still seeing double, and his head was pounding like a drum.

A bullet whizzed by his head and embedded into the concrete wall behind him. Bits of concrete stung the back of his neck, and this time, Big B put four bullets into the attacker's chest. Kirk added one to his forehead. He smiled and watched the person fall. The attacker was wearing a mask so Kirk couldn't tell if it was a woman or just a small man.

Kirk looked toward Big B and nodded. Turning, they headed toward the next block, and after ten minutes, they could see the hospital. It loomed ahead and was half lit up, but most of the lights were flickering on and off like a huge, blinking Christmas tree.

Kirk breathed in a sigh of relief; his vision was now

back to normal. The building was still sectioned off by the CDC, but now, along with the CDC vans, there were also barricades, the National Guard, and the Army surrounded the building. Looters were throwing flaming cocktails at the guards, and the guards returned fire. As they watched, the mob of fifty or so moved back and scattered like ants.

The way the city had transformed in just a few short hours amazed Kirk. He thought of the years and centuries it took to build a city. How fast it could be torn down. People would riot with the smallest of pushes and turn violent for no reason at all.

"How do we get in?" Kirk looked at the situation and was not happy about the change. *Every time I turn around, things go to pot.* Big B studied the building and pointed toward the south end of the parking lot.

"We might be able to get in through the employee entrance… Might have to grab some suits, though."

"Fine with me… You might have some trouble, though." Kirk looked the big man up and down. He had to be well over three hundred pounds, maybe even four hundred. Thick arms and wide shoulders on a tall frame made Big B look more like a monster then a man.

Kirk thought a moment and remembered his FBI badge. He still had his badge from his short time on the special taskforce, but didn't think he would be doing any more briefings for the Feds… they were a joke anyway, and they would be busy trying to keep the country from falling apart. Kirk told Big B his plan, and B smiled and nodded.

"Should work… Worst case, we go in the old fashioned way."

Kirk didn't want to know what that meant. If he was thinking about going in by force against the CDC, the National Guard, and the Army, he would have to be crazy.

Big B hunched over and headed to the rear of the building, making sure to stay far enough away to be invisible and to keep in the shadows. Kirk followed, and soon the rear entrance was in view. A sawhorse marked the barrier, and four guards in camo stood with automatic weapons.

Here we go—this should get good. Kirk pulled out his pistol and badge. Big B wrapped his arms around his gut and started coughing, dragging one foot trying to look sicker then he was. Kirk Weston puffed out his chest and stayed just behind Big B and as they got closer, the guards all snapped to attention.

"Halt! This is a restricted zone!" The tall guard stepped forward and pushed up on his helmet, exposing a gas mask. He had a thick jaw and dark eyes that were too close together, making him look like a bug.

Kirk stepped clear of Big B and held out his FBI badge. "FBI! This man is infected, and we need to get him inside. I have direct orders from Captain Jacobson…"

The four raised their weapons and stood firm. "Not another step—we will shoot!"

Kirk could feel the rage enter his face and neck. Big B started to cough and fell to the ground. He was really hamming this gig up. Still holding up his badge, Kirk stepped forward some more. "I want to talk to your superior, this is a federal matter. Do you want to be responsible for the death of the president's daughter's personal bodyguard? I am not asking you, I am telling

you—lower your weapons, or every one of you will die!"
Kirk tensed every muscle in his back and arms. He was
ready to kill if he had to.

Three of the guards let their weapon lower an inch and
they looked toward their commander. He stared at Kirk,
and then looked down at the big man on the pavement.
He looked the part, and Kirk smirked at his own quick
thinking.

"What are you going to do? Don't just stand there
like a bunch of dumb pigs, get out here and help the man
inside." Kirk let his voice grow hard and cold with self-
importance. They hesitated and Kirk pulled out his .45 and
pointed it at the commander. "I said, now!"

This move at the right time was stupid and genius all
at the same time. If he would have pulled the gun a second
earlier or one minute later, they would have gunned them
down without thinking. But because he had them all
twisted up, not sure what to do with the gun and his self-
assured body language, it gave the move an authority that
sealed the deal.

The commander's eyes flashed in anger, but he lacked
the stones to call Kirk Weston's bluff. "You heard the
man, get him inside!" Two soldiers pushed the sawhorse
aside, hung their weapons around their chests, and stepped
forward. They took Big B under his arms, and dragged
him toward the door. He was too heavy to hold up, and he
was still limp and gagging.

Kirk marched forward and shoved his ID in the
commander's face. "You see that name? You remember
it, because if you don't, next time I won't be so
understanding." Holstering his weapon, he watched the

commander read the badge name. It was signed by the director of the FBI and his face turned a brighter shade of red.

"I'm just doing my job…"

"Your job! Really, you're going to give me that line?" Kirk was mad, his shoulder hurt like a mother, and he wanted to take it out on someone. The poor commander just happened to be in his crosshairs. "Your job is to use your head for more than a helmet holder. You have no idea what is going on here, do you? This situation is so beyond your pay grade. I don't care what you think you know or what your orders are. Next time you see me coming, you better just lower your eyes and don't even look at me. You got that, commander?"

The commander opened his mouth to speak, and Kirk wondered why he didn't pull the martial law thing on him. In reality, the FBI had no power now that it had been enacted. But he knew that most soldiers had never had to actually defend against their own people. It was new to everyone. This bluff wouldn't work in a week, maybe even in a few days.

Kirk swore and spit out the side of his mouth. The commander returned to his post, and Kirk proceeded through the three-stage, plastic quarantine barrier. The CDC wore full head-to-toe yellow suits, and when they saw Kirk they rushed him to a shower area.

"Sir, we need to check you for infection. Please sit down and we will have someone draw blood." The lights flickered and Kirk looked up at the light strip and shook his head.

"It doesn't matter now, I'm here and exposed. I'll take

my chances." He flashed his badge and shoved the CDC tech aside.

"But sir, you…"

Big B was lying on a rolling bed. He sat up and brushed off the CDC worker who was trying to take his blood. "Look here, I need to talk to your supervisor."

Kirk pushed past more CDC people and stood next to Big B. "Get me your supervisor—now!" The chaos of the floor with people crying out and doctors rushing in and out of rooms all came to a stop, and the crowd stared at the two as if they were from a different planet.

Kirk whispered to Big B. "You got mine?"

Big B reached into his cargo pocket and slipped the canister to Kirk. Once he had it in his hand, he said in a hushed voice. "Get the other one to someone high up… we need them to get going on mass production. Sorry to make you go through all this."

"No prob, just get up there and save your little girl." Kirk smiled and nodded. He knew that the next few hours, and maybe even few days, for Big B would be hell. Interviews, interrogation, and suspicion.

Big B held up the silver canister and said in his booming voice. "I have the antidote, get me your supervisor!"

CHAPTER TWENTY

HOME.

The word means something different for everyone. For some, it is a warm word with feelings of joy and filled with good memories. For others, the word is confusing, something only read about or something made up on TV.

Home.

For me, it was not a place, not a house made of wood, plaster, and paint, but people. I loved my family. But I had more than one family. In one home were K and Sam, and in the other, Maria and Samson. Both real to me, real as it gets, and I had to choose.

Kreios walked a few steps away from me and his words rang in my head, bounced around like ball bearings. "You choose where home is. Where you end up is where you choose to be."

"What about the key world? What about the people I love?"

"Wherever you are will be the key, and you in all the other worlds will continue on their paths independent of you. Do not worry, they will still be loved by you."

I could not do it. I know this is the worst kind of betrayal: one of indecision. I might as well have slapped K in the face and stabbed Maria in the heart. Both decisions were not good enough to cancel out the other. Or was it because I loved both of them? Not in the same way, but both feelings were strong—strong enough to make me want to die.

I married K first, loved her and married her before I ever knew Maria. She had some sort of right to my love— first mention. But when she died, I was alone. I had to move on, to let her go. Maria didn't deserve any less, and in my mind, K was both alive and dead.

"I can't, you do it for me."

Kreios turned and gave me a stare that I would never forget. "No. You must choose. This is your life, your future. However, remember that, whatever you choose, you cannot go back. If you keep dreaming, you will draw the wrath of the Creator. It may already be too late."

"Take my hand." I reached out, Kreios took my outstretched hand, and I closed my eyes. I would not think of anyone; I would let my subconscious decide. The light and the rush of fluid that I could feel run up my arm and into my nervous system took over my thoughts, and I let love fill me from the inside out.

I knew how I felt for K, I knew it had to be her, it was always her. Even though I loved Maria, I couldn't override the true feelings and commitment for K and Sam. My mind and head hurt; I felt like a sharp knife was being stuck in my ear. I screamed out and opened my eyes.

"What's happening?" My vision was blurry and the air was cold as if someone left the window open while it was snowing outside. Where was I?

I was lying on my back on the floor of a living room. I searched my memories to find out what world I ended up in, to see if I was truly home. I searched for Kreios, but he was nowhere to be found.

Dark shadows moved at the foot of the couch, and I sat up. My head spun, and I almost vomited but held it down. I was home, in my own living room in the real world, the one with K and Sam, Isis, Kirk, and the rest of my friends. I was home. In my heart, I knew that this was the right choice. Maria would be loved, protected by me in some other life, some other time and place.

All my senses stood up on end, and the beating of my heart slowed. This sign of danger brought up all my instincts. The shadow moved again and a man stepped from the kitchen. I saw at once that it was not Kreios. Yet he moved with the same speed and fluid movements. Like silk, he walked into the living room, and I stood and searched for a weapon, anything—a gun, a knife, something to defend myself.

The voice that came from the man's mouth was not human, not even close. It creaked and squawked like a bird or like claws on concrete. "Time is up—you have been judged."

"The Brotherhood," I stepped toward the lamp to my left. It had a sturdy wooden base and would have to work for a weapon. It was all I had.

The thing nodded and rushed me. I felt the same

feeling of cold energy flow through and from my heart and out to my hands. The man, or thing, was the size of Big B, and fast. I didn't have time to grab the lamp so I waited for the beast to tackle. My hands were glowing.

No.

No...

No!

If I did the bomb thing again, here in my own house, it would kill everyone. K and Sam were sleeping upstairs. I willed my body to calm down, to undo the energy I seemed to have drawn.

Time ran out. The big man hit me in the chest with his shoulder, and we flew backward through the picture window. Glass shattered, and I could feel the impact on my back. The force of the body running at me was more than I expected. All the breath escaped my lungs, and the thing landed on top of me and was up and behind me before I could even react.

He somehow got behind me, and took his big hands, one clamped down around my lower jaw and the other held fast to the back of my head. He twisted and about tore my head off completely. I heard my neck snap before I felt it. It was as if my eardrums burst at the same time that my spine broke in four places.

Red stars flashed across my field of vision, and I dropped to the ground. The grass was wet, but I felt nothing. I knew this was the end. They won, and just like that, I was dead. I felt like a camera that had been dropped on the ground; I could only see sideways toward the feet of the beast.

I could hear K scream and run into view. Her feet were

bare, but now black crowded my vision, slowly closing in toward the center. I couldn't move. She was looking out through the broken window. I tried to force my head to move, to see her face, but no amount of will power could fix this.

Blackness. In the end, it is all just black.

———∞∞∞———

SUCKING BREATH AND SHOOTING up from a lying position made my head spin. I gulped the clean air like a starving man. My lungs burned, my eyes were watering, and I could still feel my neck stinging all the way down to my tailbone.

My mind raced and all at once, memories and conflicting thoughts converged on me. Voices from me and Kreios flooded my brain in a mass of sounds and chaos. I clutched my skull and shut my eyes, but just as I did, I remembered what had just happened.

K!

I opened my eyes and jumped to my feet. I took an attacking stance, head cocked and fists clenched, already glowing. *What is going on?*

I was in the kitchen of my house, but not the right house. This was Maria's and my house in the wrong time and place. "Oh God, please, not this… K and Sam, please!"

I felt rather then heard something behind me and I spun on my heel and saw the very same man who had just killed me in the real world, the key world. He looked up at me, and a confused look crossed his face. His jaw loosened and his eyes flashed to the dead body out on the front lawn.

Lying on the grass, surrounded by broken glass—was me. Not me, but the me of this time and place. I worked my brain through the reality of what I was seeing. It went against what Kreios had told me. He said I would assume the identity of any world I was in; I couldn't occupy the same space as myself because I was somehow subconsciously controlling the dream.

Standing up, the big man rose to his full height. I felt the energy flow from my heart again, and this time I would not mess around. But just when I thought I was ready, the man did something I never thought possible.

He split.

The man wore a thick black coat, blue jeans, and combat boots. He lurched forward but not like a man in control. Ripping from his back, a jagged wing wriggled free, followed by a tail. I stepped back and watched as the thing squirmed and clawed from the body of the big man.

It only took a few seconds, but in my mind, it was in slow motion. It was some sort of dragon-looking beast, and when the head broke free, I gasped in shock.

Demon. That was the only word to describe what I was seeing.

The two were now separate, standing next to each other. The man was breathing heavily and seemed to be gaining his strength. The demon was a full three feet taller and twice as long as the man. Its head touched the ceiling, and it had to hunch to keep from bumping it. It had a long snout, and thick, green goo dripped from its jaws.

I didn't know what this thing was, or how I was still alive and here in this time. But I knew one thing: if I let the two attack me, I would not be able to do that cool trick again.

I do not know how to control this energy, and the glowing in my hands was now so bright that it obscured my hands. My chest glowed even brighter and my shirt fell apart as if it were made of thin, dry paper.

Turning my entire mind to the feeling in my heart, I summoned my will and raised both hands toward my attackers. A beam of white light exploded from my hands and joined into one thick bolt of pure energy. I slid back. The tile floor crumbled under my feet and carved a ditch in the floor.

The energy bolt hit the man in the midsection and he popped like a watermelon. Guts and flesh blew outward, and the man crumpled to the floor in a bloody heap of flesh. This enraged the demon and he whipped his tail, catching me across the legs. I went down hard but was up again. An aura of energy burst out from my core, and I grabbed the charging demon around the throat and willed my body to react.

I felt the cold energy leave my hands and the demon's head exploded in a mess of green mush and blood. I fell to the floor, breathing heavily. I watched as the demon withered away and the remnants of it floated in a black mist. I watched in amazement as it formed into a ruby colored stone that lay on the floor, hooked to a chain. It was in the midst of the mess that was left of the man. It glowed, and all the mist disappeared.

Not cool. It must survive that way, going into that stone thing. I wondered if the man wore it around his neck like a necklace. I bet he did, it must be the connection, the way the monsters controlled their human hosts.

"What did you do?" Kreios appeared in the kitchen, a thin white glow around his body. I was no longer glowing and my palms were black and burnt. My heart thumped in my chest.

"I... I—don't... don't know." I scrambled to my feet and stood surveying the room. "Kreios, what is happening to me? This is impossible."

"You are not supposed to be here. How did you travel on your own, are you asleep?" Kreios had a hard tone laced through his voice, and it grew harsher as he looked around. "You got killed! Do you know what you did?!"

I took hold of his collar, turned him, and made him focus on me. I could feel my anger on the edge of being completely out of control. "I don't know what is going on! You tell me, Kreios. I was attacked, I was killed, and the next thing I know, I'm back here and this thing followed me or was already here. What do you want me to tell you?" I pushed him away and swore.

"I'm out! I can't do this anymore. I am hopping back and forth between worlds and realities, and I can't even control this stupid energy thing. You come along, and now I don't even know what to do or think anymore. You do what you want, but I'm done. *You got it? Done!*"

Kreios was no longer glowing. He stepped through the broken window and bent over the body of... of, well, me. He sighed. "This is not good. The Brotherhood is already here. There is no way to stop them now."

Here we go again—the Brotherhood, demons, men with crazy time travel skills, and some not-quite humans messing everything up. "What is this all about, Kreios?

No more beating around the bush. I am not moving —"

"Mark! Mark, what—" Maria stood at the kitchen doorway with a look of pure horror on her face. "Mark, what is going on… are you okay?"

CHAPTER TWENTY-ONE

REAL. JUST THE WORD brings images of things we can believe in. How can something made up ever take the place of the "real deal"? Yet in this black and white world what lives in the gray area between our ears may be real, but we shove it into the imagination department.

Supernatural, teleportation, telekinesis, and other things like this are quickly discarded as a good story or movie but not real. If it cannot be touched, felt, or seen, it must be made up—imagination.

Mooch was of this mind, but over the last few weeks, he was doubting his own thoughts. Was anything he believed real? Was it all there in front of his eyes, but like the rest of the world, he just closed his eyes to the truth? He felt like a little boy again, thinking that no one could see him just because he shut his own eyes.

Mooch stood over Isis, and when he turned and saw the thing—the presence protruding from his body and the dark sword in its hand—he came awake in a sudden jerk of painful realization.

Fear gripped his nerves as Mooch forced his mind to free itself from the reality of what he was becoming. He somehow managed to turn around, and Mooch took hold of the demon's spiked arms. He could feel warm blood run down his wrists and arms as he squeezed hard and fought with the dark, drooling thing.

"No—" Mooch ground his teeth together and pushed back on the monster, but it was like pushing against a concrete wall. No, not a wall, it was a force hard yet soft. He felt like it would vaporize at any moment and fill his lungs again, and he would be worse off than he was before.

Why was he fighting this? Wasn't he happy, wasn't he alive for the first time in his life?

"You need me! Let me in, and we will do great things. Don't you want a friend, someone who will never leave you, someone who will give you everything you want?"

"You're not real—can't be real!" Even as the words left his lips, Mooch knew he was lying to himself. Yet a part of him wanted to be a part of the thing. He would be one of a kind, someone who could do anything and be anyone. True power was—

This lapse in his resolve was all the demon needed. He reached into Mooch's chest, grabbed something, and dragged himself back in. Tail twisting and wings flapping, Mooch arched his back and screamed. The sound carried out of the room and down the hall to the elevator. The slim crack between the elevator doors and the floor caught the sound, and it flew down to the first floor where it echoed through the entire floor. Doctors, nurses, and patients stopped, and a cold shiver ran up the spines of anyone who heard. It was a subconscious thing; on some level, they all knew something was out there that was not of this world.

Mooch opened his eyes and instantly had a strong craving for meat—steak, grilled and rare. He couldn't remember what had happened or where he was. He stood up and saw dried blood on his arms and palms. No cuts were visible, no indication of where the blood came from.

The hospital room brought him back. He saw Isis and knew why he was here. Not to kill her, no, that thought was selfish and shortsighted. *We must make Kirk suffer. We must make him pay for his sins. Killing her would be too easy, too final, too short.*

Mooch felt good, real good. He stretched and raised his arms above his head and could feel the rippling muscles under his shirt. He was never a big kid, he used to get shoved into lockers, turned upside-down, and dunked in nasty high school toilets, but not now. He was a different man now.

"We are brothers. Now and forever, we are true brothers."

"Yes," Mooch whispered, "I swear to you, swear my loyalty, my devotion." He did not remember what he was or who he was talking to, but it just felt right.

The overhead lights flickered twice and went dark. Machines, once working, shut off, and the ones with batteries would last another hour, maybe two. Mooch smiled in the dark not noticing the red glow coming from under his shirt. Hung from a gold chain around his neck was a small ruby-colored stone that pulsed and hummed in the darkness. Mooch took a step toward the bathroom just as Kirk Weston walked in.

---⊗⊗⊗---

KIRK WESTON FELT HIS heart quicken. Was it hope, was it the thought that this might be over soon? He gripped the silver canister and pushed through the metal door leading to the stairwell. He didn't want to risk the elevators with the power situation; he didn't think the backup generators would last much longer.

Emergency lights were on in the stairwell, but they didn't cast much light. Kirk took the steps two at a time and was soon out of breath. He was in great shape, but not as good as he was last year when he had spent a year in captivity. Nothing to do, so he worked out every day for four to six hours.

The hall was empty, and the feeling of being along on a hospital floor made him uneasy. *Where are all the doctors? Don't they know there were people here who needed attention too?* This was just like them, look after the important ones. Just like Mark, they left him. He had a sudden fear that Isis was already dead or maybe moved to another floor.

Running down the hall, he scanned each number looking for the right one. The overhead lights flickered and went out. Kirk stopped and drew his service weapon out of habit.

Something was not right... He had an out-of-order feeling, and that scream; he could have sworn he heard someone scream as he was climbing up the stairs. It had

IN YOUR DREAMS | 193

made his skin crawl.

Kirk found room 204, and he stopped. The door was closed and not a sound came from the other side. This was not right. A bad feeling gripped his gut and twisted it into a knot. He could smell disinfectant and urine, it made him want to gag. As he opened the door, he felt rather then saw someone in the room.

The room was dark except for the red and green lights coming from the machines next to the bed. Kirk breathed in a sigh of relief when he saw Isis. He looked around the room and holstered his .45. He forgot about the feeling. All he saw was Isis.

Isis was on her back, hooked up to tubes, and her tan face had fresh boils covering both cheeks and her left eye. Kirk's breath caught in his throat. She was breathing in short, harsh gasps. Her chest heaved up and down, and her breaths sounded like water and gravel.

Kirk twisted the top off the silver canister, took out the syringe, and pulled the orange plastic cover from the needle. He did not think about the dose, didn't know if what he was giving her would kill or save. But Isis was dead already. He looked at her closed eyelids and wondered if she was too far gone already.

The soft light coming from the ECG monitor gave off enough light for Kirk to find the IV. He slipped the tip into the plastic tube and pushed down the plunger. This was it; this was what he had been looking for, what he almost died for. He set the syringe on a table next to the bed and looked at Isis as if he expected her to wake up all better. *It doesn't work like that, Kirk... give it time.*

Kirk took Isis's hand and sat down in a roll chair. He

watched her heart rate and prayed for the erratic beeping
to level out. He was not a doctor, but he knew that what
her heart was doing was not normal or good.

This life was just one problem after another. It felt
like he couldn't get a break. His first marriage ended in a
violent fight and a messy divorce. He was a good cop—
no, he was a great cop—and became a detective thinking
things would turn around for him, but instead they got
worse. His boss, the Chief, hated him and made his life a
living hell, and even though he had the highest conviction
rate on the force, he couldn't seem to get free of his past.

He did have a temper, and his need to be left alone
didn't help with keeping partners happy. He had a line of
ex-partners who wouldn't give him the time of day. Now
here he was, in the middle of a secret agency that went
around assassinating people and doing what they thought
was right for the country and the world. He not only was
now involved with them, he was helping them instead of
taking them down.

And why was he helping them? Not because he
believed in what they were doing, but because of a
woman. That's right, the great Kirk Weston, ladies man
and grumpy recluse of a man, was falling all over himself
for a woman.

But Isis was everything any man would want. She was
incredibly beautiful, but not a snob. Skin like silk, and
yet she was strong due to hour after hour in the gym. She
had black hair that seemed to be made from liquid glass,
smooth and shiny falling over her shoulders like water.
Kirk slid his fingers in between hers and wondered how
someone like her could ever like a guy like him.

He thought of her smile, the way she could kill and fight like a tiger and still be delicate and breakable. How was that possible? She not only had the looks but a personality and a heart that was true and open. She was smart and dangerous. His heart swelled. He could feel his gut ball up, and he felt like vomiting. He was going to lose her, going to watch her die before they could even try. It would be over before it even began.

"Shut up, you idiot!" Kirk twitched at the harshness of his own voice. "Stop being a baby!" He slapped himself and shook his head. If anyone saw him like this it would be the last thing they ever saw, Kirk would make sure of that.

Kirk wiped at his eyes and placed a kiss on her forehead. "I love you, Isis."

CHAPTER TWENTY-TWO

MARIA STOOD ON SHAKY legs and stared at me, or rather through me to the broken body on the kitchen floor. There was dark green and black slime everywhere, and blood was all over me and splattered all over the kitchen. Kreios was gone, and so was my body. I thanked God for that; I didn't know how I was going to explain how I was dead on the front lawn but still here.

"Maria," I took her around the shoulder and turned her away from the mess. "There was an intruder, and he attacked me." Maria was shaking, and light sobs escaped her lips. I hugged her and we sat down on the couch.

"Mark, there's so much blood and... stuff all over. Are you okay?" Her voice raised an octave, and she turned as if suddenly aware that I might have been hurt.

"I'm fine; I just need to go call the police. I need you to sit here. Promise me you will not go in there." Maria nodded, wiped her eyes, and hugged herself.

"Okay, go. I'll sit here."

The last thing I wanted to do was get the police involved, but it was something a normal guy would do if he were attacked in his home, so I had to play the part. I found my cell on the counter and flipped it open.

"Nine-one-one, what's your emergency?"

———∞∞∞———

BLUE AND RED LIGHTS flashed, bouncing off the houses in my neighborhood. I stood with my arms around Maria, and little Samson sat in the lawn throwing grass up in the air and laughing. Everyone from the neighborhood was out looking at the Appleton house and talking among themselves in hushed tones. Cell phone cameras took video and pictures that would be up on Facebook and Twitter within the hour.

"Guess we are going to be famous. We should get prime time exposure on Facebook-land for at least a week."

Maria smiled. "Yeah, just what I need. Now we'll be the family who killed a burglar."

"Hey, we don't take no crap… just try and break into my house." I saw that our neighbor Mrs. Baker was staring at us from next door. I lifted my hand and gave her a wave. She blushed, turned away, and slinked back into her house. I was sure she would go to the window and survey the scene from the behind the curtains.

Maria turned to look at me, and her eyes told me she was not buying the story I fed to the police. "Who was that man? And why was he in our house, and why was there other stuff, not just blood? Where did it come from?"

"Whoa... one at a time." I tried to lighten the mood, but she clenched her jaw. "Maria, it's hard to explain, but it seems he was a hit man who was here to kill me. He wasn't alone... I don't know what to tell you, but the other thing was not a human, it was some sort of animal."

"Well, where is the body? Did it get away?"

I fingered the red stone in my pocket and felt its smooth and cold surface. "No, I killed it, but after it died, it kind of vanished... just turned into a vapor and disappeared."

Maria looked at my chest and seemed to be thinking about how much truth was in my story. I didn't lie to her, just left out some details—some details like, *"Hey, you're not even real, just made up from my imagination. Oh, and there might even be more of you somewhere out there in other worlds that I also somehow created, and I am not your Mark, not today. Your Mark died..."*

Yeah, that would be easy to explain, no problem. The problem now was not that this was a fake, made up world, but that this was just as real as my world, or as Kreios said, "the key world." And according to him, this would become the key world if I stayed in it too long. But if I left, what would Maria and Samson do? Would they just cease to exist?

"What, baby?" Maria touched my cheek and pulled my face down. "Why the worried look? Tell me what you are thinking."

I sighed, "Just a bad night..."

My cell vibrated in my pocket and I reached for it and saw a text. I glanced up and saw Solomon coming toward me with Big B and Isis in tow. I was surprised to see

Solomon, since in my time he was dead. The sight of him filled me with joy.

Samson jumped up at the sight of Big B and ran to him yelling. "B… B… B!" Big B laughed and scooped the little boy up in his massive arms, and gave him a hug before throwing him into the air. Samson giggled and begged for more.

Solomon shook my hand and gave Maria a hug. "Good to see you, Maria. Is everyone okay?" Solomon knew we all were, and I am sure had the situation under control. My house and property were under protection, and no one entered without the WJA knowing. They had to protect their investment, after all.

"Fine, Solomon… well, as fine as we can be under the circumstances." Isis gave Maria a hug and me one, too. She smelled good as usual and didn't say anything, just smiled and stood close as if guarding me.

Big B slapped me on the back and boomed in his huge voice. "So you went and killed an intruder, did ya. Good going, man, way to show them who is boss." I couldn't help but laugh.

"Well, if you put it like that… I guess they will think twice before trying to swipe my TV in the future."

Solomon took my arm and pulled me aside. I kissed Maria and said, "Be back in a minute."

"Okay."

Solomon rubbed his well-trimmed beard and took off his glasses. "What happened?"

I doubted he didn't know already, but I humored him. "Well, it's hard to explain…"

Solomon looked over my shoulder and lowered his

voice. "Mark… we have a scan on your house and the intruder. It is human but something in there was not. We believe they were a part of each other."

I nodded. "It was a man at first, but this demon-dragon-like thing split apart from him, and I killed them both. The thing vaporized and went back into this stone." I pulled the ruby stone from my pocket and handed it to Solomon.

Solomon lowered his heavy eyebrows and examined the stone. It pulsed and hummed in an almost inaudible tone. "I will have to take this back to the lab."

"There is something else…" I wasn't sure how to tell him, but if anyone should know and if anyone could help me, it was Solomon.

"I know, Mark, we scanned you as well as the house."

"What do you mean? You know what?"

"Mark, you are dead… not you, but the you of this world. You don't even show up on our scans. It is as if you don't exist."

KIRK HAD FALLEN ASLEEP holding Isis's hand. When a sharp needle was pushed into his neck, Kirk's eyes shot open, and what he saw was an empty bed. Isis was gone! He tried to jump up, tried to move, but found that he was paralyzed.

"Remember me?" The voice came from the darkness, and Kirk could see that the monitors and equipment were now off, probably because the batteries died. The voice sounded familiar but different somehow.

"This is going to be more fun than I thought."

BIG B FELT BETTER. It was amazing how fast the antidote worked. He had been whisked away and taken to the CDC headquarters. Even after he had convinced the CDC officer that the antidote was the real deal, it still took an hour, and it was an hour they couldn't afford. Now, he was sitting in the back of a SWAT team van.

"Sir, we are almost there, but there is a roadblock up ahead." The National Guardsman held a hand to his ear. As their escort, he and one other guard held fully automatic machine guns and wore full body armor. In the van, there were also three CDC personal. One was a woman with a hard scowl on her face.

"It is going to get a little bumpy. Everyone, hold on!" Big B gripped the bar near his head. "We are going to try to drive through the road block."

Seconds later, the van crashed into something, and they tipped to the right. Big B thought they were going to go over, but the van righted itself, and gunfire pelted the outside but did not penetrate the armor.

Someone screamed, and then they leveled out and continued on. "We made it… Should be one more mile, and we will be safe inside the CDC lab." The man sitting across from him wore a green camo helmet and a thick mustache that looked like a caterpillar under his sharp hook-like nose.

Big B was breathing heavily, and he still felt weak from all the excitement of the evening. "What about the freezers with the rest of the virus?" He had relayed the information to the commander of the National Guard, and they were supposed to send some men over to transport the virus to other freezers.

"They should be on scene by now, but I have not heard anything yet," the guardsman said. He put his hand up to his earpiece again and listened. "We're here."

The back doors burst open, and a guardsman waved them down. "Move to the door and hurry, we are expecting an attack. There was a mob coming this way, and they did not look like they wanted to talk things over."

Big B stepped from the back of the armored vehicle and followed the rest of the group into a three-story brick building. Barriers were set up much like the ones at the hospital, but these also had barbed wire and many more National Guard and Army troops standing with automatic weapons. Even a .50 cal. was set up on a rotating stand.

Once inside, they were met by an older man in a white lab coat. "Is it true? Do you have an antidote?" The man was skinny, almost too skinny, and had a mess of black hair sticking up in clumps. He wore thick glasses, and his arms seemed too long for his body.

"Yes, I was infected and took it as a test. I am already feeling better, but you might want to run some more tests on me to make sure it really killed the virus." Big B handed the silver canister to the skinny man.

"Very good, my boy, very good. Come with me, please." Big B nodded to the men who made sure he got here safe and followed the funny looking man down a hall and through three security points. Each checkpoint had washing stations and x-ray scans along with armed guards.

"I didn't realize the CDC did this sort of thing." Big B pulled on cloth booties over his boots and wriggled into the full-body, bunny suit. The suit was extra-extra large but fit almost skin tight on Big B.

"We do many things here the public is not aware of: testing, and even some manufacturing. In a crisis such as this, we can produce antivirus or other drugs *en masse* throughout all our labs across the world. We have quite a large operation here, Mr. B."

They moved into a section of the building that resembled a hospital, with beds and rooms and people all in the same clean suits going about their business. Big B was led to a room at the end of the long row of doors. He lay down on the bed, and a nurse came in to take a blood sample.

"Why are you guys not in hazmat suits? Can't you catch what I have, since I might still have it?"

The skinny old man, someone had called him Les, smiled and shook his head. "No, the virus is only contagious when it is airborne. Once it is in a host, it is confined to that host. The only way to get it is to breathe it in once it is activated. You can't spread it to anyone else even if you were covered in boils and coughing up blood."

"Thanks, Doc. Good to know." Big B closed his eyes and couldn't help but wonder where Mark was hiding out. Something must have happened.

CHAPTER TWENTY-THREE

SOUNDS. DRIPPING WATER AND a hum, a motor
maybe? It was a constant thrumming from some kind of
engine, a generator, but a big one, or more than one all
going at the same time. Kirk couldn't see anything. He
couldn't tell if it was because it was dark or if his eyes
were closed.

Smells. Musty dust, oil, and warm sweat. He could
feel the heat in the room, like a sauna, only a few degrees
cooler. He could feel his shirt sticking to him and smell
his own body odor.

Taste. His mouth felt like it was small and dry. He
could taste the copper aftertaste of blood. He licked his
lips, and it sounded and felt like sandpaper on cardboard.
Hearing and taste and scent were all heightened. It was not
a downer. Something else, something meant to wake him
up.

Kirk didn't move. He could hear something beyond

the simple sounds of water and the engine. It was a ticking
sound… a nervous twitch? On top of that was heavy
breathing, but this was down by his feet, not coming from
the direction of the sporadic ticking.

Tick… tick… tick…

This was not the first time Kirk had been kidnapped.
In fact, he was beginning to wonder if this was his calling
in life. With utmost care, Kirk began to flex each group of
muscles in order to find out if he was on his back or on his
side. He couldn't tell which end was up.

*Slow… Slow… Don't give away that you're awake.
Left leg, tighten and hold for a count of 40. Right calf and
quad—flex and hold.* Kirk did this flex and hold process
with each leg and then his arms and chest and neck. He
was on his left side, head on the hot concrete.

Kirk blinked a few times once he discovered he was
blindfolded. That was good, he needed his eyes, needed
everything he could get if he was going to—

Oh, no… Isis! He remembered through his mental fog
that he was asleep and someone said something… it was
a voice of someone he knew or once knew. *What did they
say? Remember… remember what?*

Small pinholes filtered through the blindfold, and
something moved, making the little points of light move
and bend. Someone was there, standing not three feet from
the ticking something… making that insistent, annoying
sound. What was that sound? Now it was driving him
crazy. It was gone and then back… it sounded loud in
Kirk's sensitive ears.

His left arm was tingling, and his leg was on fire. They
had been numb, but with the flexing, they were waking up

and it hurt… it hurt like—

"It's not supposed to take this long." The voice, the familiar voice from the ticking man blasted through Kirk's eardrums. It took every ounce of self-control not to scream out. The ticking man was talking to himself, more like mumbling, but to Kirk he was shouting right into his ear.

"Maybe I should give him another dose…"

This was going to be his chance. The crazy ticking man was going to come over, and Kirk would have one shot to kick him, to defend himself and find Isis…

Footsteps and breathing close to his head. He could feel the little hairs on the side of his neck tickle his skin. Flexing his entire body Kirk twisted and swung his legs around. He connected with something but not the ticking man. He felt a jolt of electricity surge through his body like liquid ice.

Seconds later, he heard screaming… it was him. His throat was raw as he released a throaty scream. The pain crippling his body was worse than anything he had ever felt. It was as if every nerve was on fire and frozen at the same time.

Kirk twitched and had a mini seizure as his body fought the drugs and the overload of electricity. He passed out and was once again consumed by nightmares.

———⊗⊗⊗———

MOOCH LOOKED DOWN AT Kirk Weston and cursed under his breath. The dumb cop had tried to kick him… really? Like he would let him take him down that easy. How dumb did he think he was? Now he was going to have to wait again.

He injected more of the drug that, according to the website he bought it from, could wake anyone no matter what they were hopped up on. Of course, they had to be alive; it couldn't wake the dead. He was the dead…

He rechecked the girl and made sure his little device was working. Isis was strapped to a table and hooked up to an IV. He wanted her alive. Her rash and boils were already fading. The antidote was working, and it was going to be a shame to kill her.

No, that was not true. He was not going to kill anyone… no, he was just the watcher, the voice in the wilderness. Kirk was a killer, a heartless killer who cared more for himself then he did his so-called friends. He would do whatever it took to save his own life, and too bad for anyone who might get in his way. It would be no different now, and he was going to prove it.

Kirk muttered and turned on his back. He did not know about the cables hooked to his arms and legs. The cables were attached to a complicated pulley system. Mooch could raise and lower the detective with a flip of a switch. He was helpless to do anything about it, as he would soon find out. His right arm was in a special strap and metal rod brace. It was padded with soft cloth so it would not leave a mark on the skin.

Not that any of this mattered. There was no more police department, no more FBI or CIA. It was a new world order, and every man was the law unto himself. Who was going to stop him? He alone was sane as the rest of the city rioted and looted like a bunch of crazies.

Mooch pulled a mask over his face and placed goggles over the eyeholes. He wanted to have some fun before little Kirky knew who he was. This was going to be better than he had thought.

"Wakey, wakey." Mooch took off the black hood, and Kirk blinked in the light. His eyes searched the room like a dog looking for the food bowl.

"What—where... where am I? Where is...?" His voice was low and scratchy.

"Isis? Yes, well, she is just over there." Mooch pointed beyond Kirk's feet. Lying on the metal table was the woman. She was covered in a white sheet, and machines pumped a sedative into her bloodstream.

"She is sleeping. You will be glad to know your little antidote is working." He watched Kirk's face and was happy to see this information brought some relief. *Yes... it is good news, my bald friend.* "She would be good as new in a day or two... too bad you will have to kill her."

Kirk's head snapped toward him, and his jaw clenched. He tried to stand up, but Mooch pressed a button on a remote in his left hand, and the cables tightened and began to lift the detective off the floor.

Kirk wriggled and fought against the device, but it was no use. He hung in the air, five feet above the floor, with his arms out at his side and his feet hanging free to kick. All the weight was on his arms to hold him up. Soon, he would tire and might even pull his arms out of their sockets when his muscles gave out.

"You touch her, and I will kill you!" Kirk growled.

"Really, and how do you plan to do that? What... you're going to break the cables and jump me? I doubt that... no, you are not only going to kill her, you are going to live a long life afterward to remember what you did."

Kirk smirked and shook his head. "I don't know who you are or what you think I did to you, but this is not the way to handle this. Who are you?" Kirk changed his voice to something more calm, almost conversational.

"No, you do not get to play me. This is my show!" Mooch could feel his hands trembling. Kirk was trying to work him, as if he would talk him out of this. Kirk Weston deserved to die... he deserved to suffer, and living was worse than death. No, he would suffer for the rest of his miserable life.

CHAPTER TWENTY-FOUR

"WHAT DO YOU MEAN, I don't exist?" I knew exactly what he meant but wondered if he knew what I knew.

Solomon guided me away from the growing crowd gathering around the crime scene. His voice was low, and I had to strain to hear him above the sirens and the sounds of my neighbors talking about the "murders." "Mark, I don't know what is going on, but I fear it has something to do with your dreams, your glimpses."

I didn't know how long it would take the police to figure out there was a second attacker. I could feel my gut tighten, and a warm, uncomfortable feeling crept up my throat. "Solomon, I know I can trust you, but this thing... What I mean to say is, I'm not supposed to be here, not like this, I mean."

Solomon stared at me with hard eyes and didn't blink for a breath. "Okay, what are you talking about?"

"Look, the police are only going to find one body

in there… I am going to have to make up some story of getting attacked by one guy, but the blood they find will prove there were two attackers, and now there's a missing body …" I took a deep breath and figured that it didn't matter what he thought, I had to tell someone.

"I am dead, Solomon. I killed myself." I couldn't help a tight laugh. "Okay, not me but…hmmm. You know my glimpses? Well they are not just dreams or something in my head. I am from some other dimension… another time that runs parallel to this one. I dreamed and woke up here, with you and this." I waved my hand toward my home. Solomon didn't say anything.

"I woke up and I was staring at myself being killed by this monster. A man, but a beast. When I killed him… er… it, well, it turned into a dark vapor and went into this stone."

Solomon looked at the stone with renewed interest. "You saw yourself die? So where is… the other you?"

"Kreios took my body before Maria could see it. It would have been too much for her."

"Kreios?"

"Oh… uh… never mind. He's a friend, but not like us. He's the one helping me to try to figure this out. I know how it sounds, but I need help. You're dead in my world, Solomon, and K and Sam are alive, and Maria's just a secretary at my old job. You see what's going on? This is crazy, but I can't stop it—I stood there and saw me—I saw myself die, and it was real."

Solomon put a hand on my shoulder. "It is okay, we will figure this out. This would explain why you don't show up on any of our scans. It is as if you are not real, at least not in this world."

I remembered what Kreios said. "Kreios said something about a key world. He said that if I stay here too long, this would become the key world... does that mean anything to you?"

Solomon seemed to think and nodded. "Well... if what you say is accurate, this world as you say is or has been created by you. We did not exist, but once you dreamed it, we became. Now that you are here, and especially now that your other self is dead, this could become the key, or the center, world."

"What does that mean for K and Sam? What happens to me on the other side?"

Solomon shook his head and massaged his temples. "I am not sure... I need to get you back to the Merc building and run some tests. I think the others will just keep going on as if nothing happened... live their lives and your awareness would just be here instead of there."

I shook my head and knew that choosing was no longer a matter of what I wanted but what was right. K was my wife, she was first, and she did not die, not for real. My tongue felt dry, and I had a bad headache. This was not natural... this kind of thing was not supposed to even be possible.

My left arm tingled, and I could hear something far away. It seemed as if someone were singing in my ear... It was not anything more than a whisper, as if someone were trying to break past the walls of this reality and reach out to me. Suddenly, I felt alone. How could one man deal with all this? I had no one, and yet everyone.

"Mark... Mark, look at your hands..." Solomon

sounded frantic, I looked down to my hands, and they were transparent. I could feel my heart beat up into my head, and the pounding made my head feel like it was going to explode.

Solomon pulled me away from my house and half-dragged, half-carried me around the back of the house across the street. Mrs. Combs lived there with her husband. How did I know that?

"Listen to me, Mark." Solomon had me on the ground, and I could barely make out his face. The world was dissolving, as if in any second, it would cease to exist.

"You have to stop this, Mark, find out how to stop this and…" His voice trailed off, and I saw that it was not me that was disappearing but him.

At that moment, time stood still, or so it seemed. I watched as Solomon broke apart into puzzle size pieces and the side of the two story house crumbled and hung in the air as if gravity were just a theory. The tree in the back yard scattered, and I saw that the pieces of everything turning in a circle—swirling like a tornado, and they were picking up speed.

The house, lawn, trees, Solomon, the garden hose, and the little garden gnome all mixed into one mass of color and the pieces clinked together, sounding like metal… as if someone just dropped a pocket full of coins.

My hands were gone now, and I saw that my assumption that the world was disappearing was now 100 percent true. I was going, too. White light filled the center of the twisting circle, and I looked over my shoulder. The ground was gone, and all around me, the entire street was moving in a dance. I closed my eyes, not wanting to see

Maria, or what was left of her. The only thing I realized later was that no one seemed to be in pain. It was all dry— no guts or blood, just dry pieces of metal were frozen as if they just stopped, as if someone had pulled the plug to a video game.

I smashed my eyes shut, and even though I did, the hot, white light seemed to be on the inside of my eyes. I didn't want to see anymore, I didn't want this life anymore. I prayed that I would wake up, that I would end up back home. But where was home? Did I even have a home anymore? I was lost.

———⊗⊗⊗———

KIRK HURT. HE TESTED his bonds, but he knew from experience that he was not going to get out. *I should teach a class. "How to Get Kidnapped: The surefire way to get into trouble," by Kirk Weston.*

He pulled anyway. The cables just gave him enough room to move a little but not enough to scratch his nose, which itched like a mother.

Kirk wondered what time it was, and what day it was. He didn't know how long he was out, but the man in the mask was gone, and the empty room was still hot as a sauna and quiet. He blinked and tried to focus, and he discovered that he was hanging. Five feet off the ground. His arms were stretched out their full length, and his legs were stretched in the same manner. He tried to curl his arms, but all it did was give him a cramp. This contraption was crazy. What kind of nut job thought of this crap?

Kirk licked his dry lips. Small noises felt amplified in his head as if his eardrums had been stripped raw. It was the sound of sandpaper on wood. He turned his head. He tried to look behind him, but all he saw was the tail end of a metal table. Strapped to the table were two beautiful feet.

"Isis!" Kirk croaked out her name, and that hurt even more. It felt like the back of his throat was bleeding. "Isis… Isis… are you okay?"

No response.

Twisting as far as he could, Kirk strained his neck. He saw to her shin but could not see any more. He knew it was Isis; the color of her skin, it was a mix of coffee and milk. He watched as long as he could hold the uncomfortable pose to see if she moved. Even a twitch, something to let him know that she was alive. He could feel hot tears creep up into his eyes but he forced them down.

He wouldn't cry. He was a man, and this was not the time to become all emotional. *Come on, buddy, you're a jerk and a no good cop from Detroit. You eat fear for breakfast and drink lead for dessert!*

Sweat dripped down his back, and off the tip of his nose. He smiled and tugged on his wrist straps. The sweat made them slick. He pulled and thought he might just be able to break free, but the strap holding his wrists and ankles were padded, and the padding soaked up the sweat. Useless.

Kirk cursed and started kicking and screaming even though it made his throat burn. After a moment, he gave up and sucked in the hot air, already exhausted. *Think, detective, don't get mad but think. You're a pro, you are the best cop that ever walked the streets. This is some psycho, some skinny runt that thinks he can mess with...*

Kirk focused on the room. It was about ten feet across and twelve or fifteen feet deep. Plaster walls, old and stained. A warehouse, maybe? A big metal door stood at the far end, and it, too, was covered with rust and grime. The floor was concrete, and equipment littered the ground. Tall, metal, storage racks were stacked up against the walls.

The parts seemed to be engine pieces... but big. Maybe from big rigs or a train. A train—that had to be it—they were in an old train warehouse. He saw a thick extension cord running from under the door and past him to the table where Isis was. He looked up and saw the hanging light with a single bulb, not a small one, but the big kind that hummed and took forever to turn on.

Okay, this might work. Got parts, maybe something to use for a weapon, but first he had to get free. Kirk looked for the camera. There had to be a camera. He located it high up above the door. It was staring right at him with a little red light glowing ominously.

An unexpected sound about gave Kirk a heart attack. Isis coughed and wriggled as she awoke. Kirk called out and twisted again, trying to see her. "Isis! Are you there? Talk to me..."

He could hear her moving and groaning, but she didn't say anything. Maybe he had her gagged, maybe he cut her tongue out. The thought of someone else touching her enraged Kirk.

"Isis!" Kirk screamed, and the sound reminded him of someone who had lost everything and didn't have anything to hide. He had no more pride, no self respect, no

selfish desires. All he wanted was for her to live… and to kill the skinny little creep who had hurt her.

Isis spoke in a harsh voice, low and strained. "I'm okay… just got a killer headache, but okay." Kirk breathed in and let out a long sigh.

"Thank God."

"What about you?" Her voice sounded better this time.

"Oh, great, just hanging out."

Isis managed a small laugh. "I see that."

"How are you feeling? The antidote… I got it for you, I found it!"

Three seconds passed, and she answered. "Great. I feel good, come to think about it. Thank you, Kirk."

The sound of a bolt unlocking brought Kirk's head around, and a masked man entered the room. It was the skinny little cuss Kirk was going to kill. "We are awake… Good, now we can have a little chat."

CHAPTER TWENTY-FIVE

OH MAN, THIS WAS the best feeling ever. Beyond the high of breaking into a so-called secure website or controlling the transportation department's payroll, this was better… like holding a magnifying glass over a helpless ant. Only this ant was not helpless, and that made it so much more fulfilling.

Mooch didn't think the annoying, backstabbing detective knew who he was, and the reveal would be amazing. He would wait for the perfect time and *bam!* The look on Kirk Weston's face would be epic.

"You've been hanging out with the wrong crowd, hacking into the wrong networks, and killing the wrong people."

Kirk searched his mask, and a look of confusion crossed his face. This was even better then he imagined.

"Listen…" Kirk said. The guy was going to try to reason with him. Really, after betraying him, after treating him like a used up convict, he dared to talk him down?! "I don't know what you want, but we can talk this out. Just leave the woman alone, you can have me, but please let her go. She has nothing to do with this." His voice was ragged, and guttural.

"I can *have you*? I already have you, and you have made your first mistake, Mr. Weston. You let your feelings overrun your reasoning. You just let me know that you care for her…" Mooch pointed toward Isis. "More than yourself… interesting, I didn't think it was possible."

So this was the one who took his place, the one who was able to break Kirk Weston. Isis somehow got through his thick skull, and down into his black heart.

Mooch waited for Kirk to protest, but he did nothing. Just like him, he let the chips fall where they would, but he would do whatever it took to keep himself alive. He was like a rat, he would claw and drown anyone or anything in his path just to keep his own head above water.

"What do you want? Money?"

"Money cannot buy happiness."

"I can get you whatever you want. Just tell me."

"What I want, I can't have. What I want is gone, never to be replaced, and there is nothing you can do or say to fix this little pickle you're in. Just accept your fate and the fate of your girlfriend!" Mooch spit out the word girlfriend remembering his girlfriend, the one Kirk killed—the one he turned against him.

Isis held her head up off the table and was watching him with sharp black eyes. He was worried about her, not that he would let on that she scared him. But she was a killer in every sense of the word, and that made him nervous.

Mooch walked toward her, and on his way grabbed the edge of a small, rolling metal table. Placed on top were different tools, pliers, and screwdrivers in various sizes. Kirk cursed and yelled at him, trying to twist to see what was going on.

"What are you doing? Leave her alone. If you touch her, I will kill you!"

"Too late," Mooch muttered under his breath, "you already did."

FUNNY THE THINGS I remembered at the oddest times in my life. I watched a very real world break apart right in front of my eyes, and all I could see and hear was the sound of metal. It was as if little pieces of glass and steel were bumping into each other and the sound brought up a past memory that I was not sure was mine or one implanted into my head as a child.

I was eight or nine and stood in the woods holding a rifle. It was a .22, and I was hunting with my dad. I could not bring up his face, and to this day I do not remember what he looked like, just the sound of his voice.

I was alone, told to stay put and watch. If I saw a deer, I was to shoot. I wondered if he really thought I could kill a large deer with such a small weapon, but he taught me to shoot, and I knew that I would aim for the deer's eye.

The smell of wet pine trees filled my nose, and the cold air made my breath hang in front of my face looking like a small cloud. Time seemed to be a distant memory here, as if, in the woods, the clock did not tick, and the hands stopped their rotation. I could feel my father's presence somewhere behind me but didn't see him.

I shifted the rifle from my right arm to my left. I checked the chamber, and that same metal-on-metal sound filled the silence. A squirrel scrambled up the side of a tree, and his nails gripping the bark sounded like Velcro ripping. He saw me and squalled in protest.

I glanced up at him and listened to the leaves as they fell down like light snowflakes. They landed without a sound, and I took a long deep lungful of the wooded air. The incessant squirrel would not let up, and I knew that in this wood, he was the alarm bell, the one who warned the others who lived there of an intruder. I swung my rifle around without a thought, and squeezed the trigger. A quiet *pop* sent him to his death, and he landed in a bed of fresh leaves. That hushed his warnings.

I didn't worry about the shot scaring any deer. It was hunting season, and the sounds of gunfire were all around, in and out of the draws and valleys, making popcorn noises. My .22 was very quiet and would go unnoticed.

I could now strongly smell the urine of a deer, or maybe an elk. It came up the valley and wafted across my face, and I turned from the hiding spot in which I was crouched down, waiting and watching. I spotted a large whitetail standing at attention not fifty yards from me. Between him and I was a large thicket of scrub brush, or what we called "buckbrush." He did not see me, but the shot at the squirrel must have brought him up and out of his bed.

Bringing up the rifle with the care of a surgeon, I

looked through the scope and waited, letting my breathing
calm to a slow, in and out motion. The buck had a nice
rack, but I didn't care; I was here for my dad, I was here
for the kill. Something about the hunt filled me with
something I could not put into words. It was him and me.
No longer would the squall of a mad squirrel or the snap
of a branch keep me from winning this battle of wits. My
dad said it was fair this way. If I missed, the prey would
escape; if I didn't make the perfect shot, I would lose and
the deer would grow in wisdom for the next time.

The quiet and the natural sounds of the woods calmed
the deer after a full ten minutes. I held firm even through
my arms were aching and my back hurt down low. I did
not let my brain command my body to move for I knew if
it did, I would go home empty-handed.

The buck had a thick coat of tan, and a clean white
belly and neck. He stood with ears up. He sniffed the
air, and his left ear flicked. He took a step forward, and I
waited. I had to see his eye, to have a second to make the
shot, but up until now, a thicket had been blurring most of
his body and head.

The buck put his head down, most likely smelling his
own scent. He had forgotten the *pop* of the rifle. Must
have chalked it up to his imagination. He would not be
making that mistake again, or any other.

The buck took three more steps from the cover of the
buckbrush, and his head came into clear view. I closed
one eye and placed the crosshairs a quarter-inch above his
right eye. I squeezed the trigger, and a .22 bullet tore free.
Before the sound reached the buck's brain, the bullet was
mangling its way through, tearing skin and forcing the

bone and brain matter to collide. The bullet smashed and spread as it hit the other side of the buck's skull. It exited with a spray of blood and brain.

I pulled another shot off so fast that the sound from a distance would make any hunter swear he only heard one shot. The second bullet I placed an inch to the left of the first. I did not want to chance the deer running and making more work for me and my dad as we tracked a mindless deer through the woods.

The second shot did not kill the buck—it was dead on its feet already—but it didn't hurt to make sure. I waited with gun still ready, looking through the scope, waiting for the buck to fall. It did. Legs buckled, and it jerked its head up as if that would help to clear its vision. The buck fell and made a loud, deep thud as it hit the earth. I stood up and walked to the deer, looking to my left and to the right for any sign of other hunters. In these woods, if I moved without hunter orange I might get shot if a half-drunk hunter mistook me for deer. Dad said it was better to be invisible then to be seen.

The buck twitched its leg, and after a few minutes, it fell silent. I felt a sort of pride knowing that I killed this huge beast with a little .22. I was underage, and it wasn't legal to use this small of a gun hunting deer anyway, but dad was weird about that way. He figured he was an adult and could decide for himself. Besides, he said the only reason they didn't allow such a small caliber weapon was because most people couldn't hit the broad side of a barn, so the bigger the better...

I OPENED MY EYES, still smelling the gunpowder and
the fresh clean mountain air in my lungs to find that it
was morning. I was in my own bed, and somehow K was
next to me. I turned over to see her form under a thin satin
sheet and watched her deep breathing. Her back was to
me, and her blonde curls lay across her shoulders and fell
on her pillow, transforming into a halo. I felt burning tears
fill my eyes, and I let them fall down my cheeks. How
could I ever even think of leaving her, even in my dreams?

What had I done to deserve this lot in life? Was it not
enough to be gifted and expected to handle the dreams?
Did they have to be more then dreams and glimpses? Did
they have to be real?

I couldn't break away from watching her. I moved
closer to K and drew her to my chest. She sighed in her
sleep, and I held her and buried my face in her hair.

This life is full of moments where it's all worth it—all
the pain and trials and troubles. This was one of those
times. I was home, I was finally home. I didn't know how
everything would turn out, but I knew that I was here now,
and no amount of worry would ruin this moment.

"I love you, K," I whispered as I felt her warmth. She
snuggled closer to me and went on dreaming. I hoped her
dreams were better than mine.

CHAPTER TWENTY-SIX

IT WAS SO HOT… stifling and humid, and it was getting on Kirk's nerves. The masked man was behind him and preparing to do something to Isis. The thought of what might happen brought Kirk into an overpowering rage.

He twisted and squirmed, pulling at his restraints, but all it did was wear him out and possibly give his captor some weird kind of pleasure. "You sick twisted freak! I swear to God, if you touch her, I will kill you… Nothing will stop me, not even death! You hear?"

A small chuckle boiled his blood even more. Red flashes crossed his vision, and he had to force himself to calm down. *Keep this up, and you will pass out and be no good to anyone.*

"I bet you want to know what I am going to do. Yes, shall we let him see?" Kirk could imagine the sicko asking Isis as if they were old friends.

The masked man walked around and left the room

to return moments later with a full-length mirror on a wooden frame. He stood it up in front of Kirk and positioned it so he could see the table. Isis lifted her head and looked him in the eyes. Something in them chilled Kirk to the bone. She was not there... not really. Her dark eyes were flat, deadly. She was in the killer zone.

Kirk had seen this look before. Each time it sent his arm hair up on end, and he could feel his gut knot up in a tight ball. This was Isis the assassin, Isis the killer.

"There, now you can enjoy the show. Shall we begin?" The kidnapper scratched his face, rubbing the mask up and down, and groaned. "This thing itches like crazy..."

"Then take it off. If you're going to kill us, what does it matter if we see you?" Kirk instantly regretted saying anything. He might have just sealed their fate.

"In time... all will be clear in time. Besides, I am not going to kill you, Kirk Weston. You are going to live." He laughed, the sound muffled in the cotton of the ski mask.

Kirk wished he could have just one hand free, just one, little hand so he could free himself and choke the perp. He would do it with his bare hands. He could hear his windpipe collapse and feel his spine snap under his fingers. It brought some relief. He stared at the tray filled with nasty looking tools.

Think detective, you have to do something. Use your head, and get out of this!

The masked man picked up a fat chopping knife. It had a short blade, but was tall and curved. Most people used it to chop veggies or meat in the kitchen. In his hands, it looked evil, and Kirk could feel the future closing in on him.

This couldn't be happening... this had to be a dream, some sort of sick joke. But as he watched, he got a sinking feeling deep down in his chest. "Please don't do this... you can do whatever you want to me, but leave her alone!" His own voice sounded pathetic even to him, but he was not sure how to stop this crazy—

"Are you a loyal friend, Mr. Weston?" He was fingering the blade, turning it over in his hands. He turned and looked at Kirk in the mirror.

"Yes."

The kidnapper went rigid and screamed so loud that both Kirk and Isis flinched. *"Liar!"*

The heavy knife came down and severed the last three fingers of Isis's left hand. Kirk and Isis did not move—not a scream, not a sound—only the heavy breathing of the man with the knife. It was not real... this was a dream; it could not end like this.

Blood moved down the metal table and began to drip down to the floor. The sound rang in Kirk's ears. Drip... drip... drip.

Kirk, for once in his life, was speechless. No words came to his mind, no smart comebacks or remarks. Isis was now breathing harder, and the blade hit the tray with a *clang*. Picking up a bowl of a clear liquid, he took Isis's hand and dipped it in the bowl. The red blood colored the bowl, and Isis flinched.

Soon the wounds sealed over. The liquid dried like wax, and the kidnapper picked up the three fingers and walked over to Kirk. He stayed behind him and held them up in the mirror. "Why did you do it, Weston? Why did you take her fingers?"

Kirk was shaking now, and tears were streaming down his cheeks. They burned, and his voice was shaking more than his body was. "Dead... you're—"

"Yeah, yeah, I'm dead, and you are going to kill me... You just hurt your little girlfriend because you lied. I wonder what else you will do to her?"

Tossing the fingers at the mirror, the masked man turned and walked out of the room. Kirk stared at the red smears on the glass. He knew at that moment that he was not going to make it out alive. This was not in his control, not anymore.

"*LIAR!*" MOOCH POWERED THE knife down with everything he had. He knew that he could do anything to Kirk and not really hurt him. But this would hurt him, this would make him feel the pain he had caused him.

The crunch and the sound of metal meeting metal sounded in the quiet room. The silence afterward made it all worth it. *He dared to lie to me, dared to play me like he used to... not this time, Kirky, never again.*

He sat in a high-backed chair, staring at the computer monitors remembering the feeling. It was scary and yet fun all at the same time. A feeling of total power flowed though his blood, making him an addict. Was this how it felt to be God? To be able to control everything, to do whatever, with no one to say "no" or "you can't do that"?

Mooch opened up another can of pop and logged into the downed network. Power, transportation, gas, and water were all down worldwide. It was simple, really. One well-made worm and the whole thing came down in a chain reaction of events. One power plant would try to aid the downed one and overload, and so on.

It had only been 24 hours, but the country was in a panic, and there was nothing to stop the end. Not even Mooch could stop it now… not even God himself.

MORNING WAS ALWAYS MY favorite part of the day. It was after all the fears of the night, and the cares of the day had not yet reached out to take a hold of my heart. The day was new, fresh, and waiting for me. I opened my eyes not knowing where I would be or when I would be.

I didn't know what to expect or what to think anymore. My life was a series of twisted events and choices all leading to random places and times. How was I supposed to live a normal life? How was I supposed to be a husband and father with this cloud hanging over my head?

I lay on my back, knowing I had to do something. K was sleeping next to me. She seemed to always be my anchor to reality—to what was real. I knew I needed to stay, to live here, but how could I not dream?

I thought of Kreios, of his healing and appearance into my life. The book and all that it held—could that be the key? This book, my book, had to be found. If it could control my life, if that was the key, I had to find it and maybe, just maybe, fix the mess.

Closing my eyes, I could feel the glimpse so close to the surface, it was there reaching out to me, and I knew that there was one thing I could do. I could destroy the other worlds. I had the key, I *was* the key, and like Kreios said, I created them, so I could destroy them. But there were so many, hundreds, maybe thousands. How could I go to each one? It would take forever.

I turned over and kissed K on the cheek. She stirred and sighed. I could smell her skin and the sweet scent of her hair. This was what I was fighting for, her and what we had, our life together. Sam and what one day she might become.

It was so easy now, like taking a leap into a pond. The ripples went out, and in them were worlds upon worlds.

CHAPTER TWENTY-EIGHT

"KREIOS!" I COULD FEEL wind on my face. It smelled of car exhaust and a mixture of food vendors and sweat. "*Kreios!*" I had my eyes open, but the street around me was all out of focus. It reminded me of dreams where I couldn't clear my eyes, and no matter what I did, I was looking through a fog.

The fog lifted, and everything was clear. At once, I knew I was not in my time. New York City was running at full speed, and the sidewalks and streets bustled with people, cabbies, and all the sounds that came with the center of the world. I smiled in spite of myself, and the feeling of being home overwhelmed me.

I did not see or feel Kreios, he was not there, and then in the same instant, he was at my side as if he just walked into this reality. I looked at him, and he stared past me to the city beyond.

"We have a problem." I was not sure how much he

knew, but I figured he knew enough.

"Yes." Again his lack of vocabulary made me uneasy.

"Do you know what happened when you left me? The whole thing crumbled... I mean, literally crumbled. The trees, the people, and I faded and woke up back home.

Kreios looked at me with a curious stare. He seemed to be thinking about what I just told him. "This has never happened before. But in a way, it makes sense... you created that reality and once you or your other self died, it no longer had anyone to keep it all together."

"Yeah, that makes perfect sense!" I was failing to keep control of my temper. "How does any of this make any sense? This is the most screwed up thing ever... I mean, I really can't think of anything more screwed up."

"That could be the key... In fact, if we let the Brotherhood kill you off one by one, that could help us. There are too many for you to kill on your own, and we are running out of time."

"Let them kill me? What about me... the real me?"

"I will protect you. But we need to fix this dreaming thing... if you keep it up, there will be no stopping it without killing you." His matter-of-fact tone scared me a little.

I had not thought about Isis and Kirk, but they came to mind now. I had been so consumed with my own plight that I had forgotten that, in the real world, things were getting bad. Isis might be dead by now, and I was supposed to be helping them.

"Do not worry about them. Things will take care of themselves if you do what is needed." I hated him reading my mind like that. *But you know that... Don't you?*

The corner of his mouth rose a half inch, and I walked toward a newspaper stand to see where and when I was. The stand was painted red, and the paint was peeling around the corners. I pushed in the correct change and took out a paper. The headline stated that the country was now officially out of the "Great Recession." *Wonderful... glad we are past all that. Funny how they think it is all over just because* they *say so.*

The date was July 19, 2012. Perfect… I was beginning to not like the number 19; it seemed to be cropping up everywhere.

I looked up and down the street and noticed that things here were a little different. A few of the cars were of a type I'd never seen before, and some of the brand names were different.

"Why are we here?" I asked.

Kreios seemed to consider. He always seemed to think before he spoke. Every word was thought out, and he never wasted them. "You have created this reality before… this is not a new one, you came here. I think we are here for the book."

The book. I could feel something, as if a force were calling to me, and every time I turned around, it was there. "But how can it be here… wouldn't it be in the key world?"

"Maybe this was the key world at one time." I considered this, and the thought gave me chills. How could I be sure that my life with K was the original key— the true world and the life I was supposed to live?

"You choose your own path. No one can make that choice for you. If you are meant to be with K and Sam, you will be with them."

"Somehow that does not make me feel better. Anyway, if I think about it anymore I am going to drive myself crazy. Who knows, maybe I already am."

I rolled the paper up and tucked it under my arm and said, "So, how do we find this book?"

"We don't. It will find us. Do you remember who you are here?"

It was an odd question, but I could now remember who I was. This life and the memories I had here flooded my subconscious and I knew what choices led me to this path. "Yes, Maria and Kale. I'm married, and here, Solomon is dead." The memory made me sad, I missed him. He was like a father to me.

"Good, now you need…" his voice trailed, off and I looked at his face. He was staring behind us at something. I turned and saw two men working through the crowd. They were huge, over six-foot-six and built like linebackers. I could feel a presence coming from them, and at once I knew who they were.

The Brotherhood.

KIRK WESTON WAS A man of action. He liked to do and was not much for talk. He was of the old-school way that did, and asked for forgiveness later. He was used to being in control, but the last few years, starting with his divorce and his first kidnapping, things just kept happening to him, forcing him to live outside of his control.

He hated the feeling, but he could deal with it. But

now that Isis was hurt, now that this sick freak had cut her, Kirk was not able to deal with it anymore. He snapped inside. Something went wrong in his head that he knew was the only thing keeping him alive.

He wanted nothing more than to hurt the man who had hurt Isis. He didn't want to just kill him, but he wanted to hurt him. Visions of pulling fingernails and cutting his eyelids off and other unimaginable things filled his head.

Isis was sleeping. He could see her in the large mirror. She was beautiful and had been through so much already. She just made it through a near death experience due to a virus and now she was here, and it was all Kirk's fault.

He knew that he would die here, but he also knew that this sick freak wanted to make him suffer. He had something against Kirk, and wanted to keep him alive to live out his life in torment.

Kirk thought about this for a long time and began to work out a plan. He was willing to die, but he wanted to save Isis. She deserved to be free, deserved better then death because of him.

The gizmo he was strapped to prevented escape, but this little plan did not require his escape… only his death.

Kirk gritted his teeth and took one last look in the mirror… this time he did not look at Isis. He looked into his own eyes. They were full of life, and something in them gave him the courage he needed. They were fierce, evil, and set. He was going to look inside himself and find the beast that lived there. He needed him now, needed to set him free.

"*Argh!*" Kirk Weston filled his lungs from the bottom and lurched and struggled, letting out a blood-curdling scream. Isis jerked awake and lifted her head to stare at Kirk. Cursing and screaming he pulled on his restraints and could feel his shoulders pulling. The socket on his left shoulder popped loose, and a surge of searing pain shot up his neck.

This was what he needed to keep it up, and he let out a fresh yell. This one sounded like a man going out of his mind. He kicked and twisted, meaning to tear his own limbs off if that was what it took.

A heavy door burst open, and the masked man entered and stood looking up at him. "What are you doing?"

Kirk fought an invisible foe. He rocked his head back and forced it forward to bite down on his tongue. Blood filled his mouth, and he spit it out in a gush. "*You want me? Come and get me!*" He screamed like a maniac and thrashed, pulling his other shoulder out of its socket. The pain now was so overwhelming that it was almost numbing. Kirk took this as his chance to overwork his heart and hoped he would pass out or have a heart attack.

"Stop it!" The skinny masked man hollered. But his voice was drowned out by Kirk's screams. The kidnapper looked around as if, for once, not sure of what to do.

Light, bright white and red stars filled Kirk's vision. He yanked and kicked his legs, trying to pull free, but it was no use. The only way he was getting out was if the kidnapper let him out.

Now the cables squalled and the pulleys strained under the pressure. Kirk could no longer hear his own voice. He was rocking back and forth, and the man in the mask was yelling something to him, but he kept on. He twisted and yanking his head back, he arched his back spewing blood and profanity.

A dark force took over his mind as he yelled and thrashed. This was what he wanted: to break his own mind, to wreck his own body. Thick veins popped out in his neck and arms. Muscles bulged and flexed as he fought himself. He opened his eyes wide and laughed in the face of his kidnapper.

"Fool! You can't take me, I will take myself!" Strange giggles burst from his lips, and he clenched down on his lip and spat the fresh blood at his foe.

MOOCH COULDN'T BELIEVE WHAT he was seeing. Kirk Weston was now officially off the map. He must have snapped and gone crazy. Mooch was disappointed. He had wanted this, but not so soon. He imagined a week or more of fun with Kirk and his girl, but the guy had gone and lost it already.

"Stop It!" He was getting worried someone might hear. Kirk was screaming, and the sound was like nothing he had ever heard. It was not the sound of a man… it was something different, and it sent chills up Mooch's spine.

He stood still in awe as the detective pulled and twisted. He bit down on his tongue and spit out a mouthful of blood. Mooch stepped back a step even though he was out of spitting distance.

"*You want me? Come and get me!*" Kirk sounded like a demon rather than a man. Mooch knew what one sounded like, after all.

The thought crossed his mind that he could be faking, trying to get him close and attack him. But no man would pull his own shoulders out of their sockets and bite his own tongue. Mooch screamed at him, but the sound was drowned out. He couldn't believe this loser was going out like this.

Then the idea occurred to him. Kirk was not getting out, no, he was secure, but he could have a heart attack or something. It would do no good to kill him, not yet; he had so much more to tell him. He wanted to kill him with the knowledge that his girl was dead and that it was him who killed her. He wanted him to know who had done this to him.

What if he managed to kill himself? He was making a go at it. Mooch could see thick veins bulging in his forehead and running in cords up his neck. They were throbbing, and just as he took another step forward.

Holy crap, he was going to kill himself. Kirk wretched and didn't stop screaming out in that crazy scary voice. Mooch could feel the fingers of fear creep up in his stomach.

"Fool! You can't take me, I will take myself!" He bit down on his own lip and a spurt of blood shot up. Kirk spat but missed him. He started giggling, and it sounded like a cat fighting with an owl. His eyes bulged, and he grinned with a bloody smile. Mooch jerked backward.

He turned to get the tranquilizer gun from the other room when Kirk vibrated and jerked like he was hooked to a thousand volts of electricity. His eyes rolled back in his head, and blood ran from his mouth and nose.

Mooch stared in horror as his revenge and his plan to torment Kirk Weston vanished right before his eyes. "Oh no you don't... you are not going to die that easy."

He rushed forward and grabbed the control to the cable system. He pushed the down arrow button, and the cables began to spin as he lowered Kirk to the hard, concrete floor.

Kirk Weston lay still, either dead or passed out. Mooch was sweating, and he cursed himself for keeping it so hot in here.

Rushing forward, he almost slipped in the blood and vomit but managed to keep his footing. He was blind with rage as he imagined Kirk Weston dead on the floor. His death would make for the ultimate failure. He would live on knowing that his old friend would never know who had won.

Mooch fell to his knees and pushed his fingers to Kirk's neck. He waited and cursed when he felt nothing. He leaned over and pulled off his ski mask and put his cheek in front of his mouth hoping for some air to tickle his skin. Again, he felt nothing.

Kirk Weston was dead.

CHAPTER TWENTY-NINE

KIRK WESTON HAD DONE some stupid things in his day, but this took them all, hands down. He had worked himself into a heart attack and forced himself to an early death. He saw a bright light and rolled his eyes. Really? A white light... come on, this was stupid.

He didn't believe in God, and the idea of heaven or hell was just not something he had ever considered. Now he was not so sure. He couldn't see anything but the big dumb light.

Cold pressed against his back, and he could feel some feeling begin to filter into his limbs and body. All at once, a flowing, sharp pain ran the length of his body. It ended in his head, and everything else ached and throbbed. It felt like he had stood on the highway and gotten hit by a semi truck.

His body hurt so badly that it almost didn't hurt. Too much information was overloading his system. His nerve endings were fighting for brain space; they were all trying to have the same airtime and clogging, and his brain just shut the door and waited to reset.

He couldn't remember where he was or what happened, but he now knew that he was not dead. A voice, muffled and far away, hit his eardrum, but he couldn't make it out. It sounded like someone he knew, but he couldn't place him.

The memory bank kicked in, the white light faded, and his vision began to clear. His eyes were open, staring out into eternity and seeing their future—good or bad. Kirk could see that he was on the floor, and someone was standing over him, but turned away.

He remembered it all. His blood pumped and boiled, but he did not trust his arms and legs to react. All he knew was pain and hate.

Mooch turned, and Kirk knew everything he needed to know with the sight of the kid. He was alive and was angry with him for leaving him. But Mooch was not himself, and now everything made sense. The rolling blackouts, the stock market going down… maybe even the virus. It all had the mark of an expert hacker… one with a vendetta.

However, Kirk didn't care about his hurt feelings or what evil he assumed the mean old world had subjected him to. He had hurt Isis, had cut off her fingers, and that and the threat of death was unforgivable. This and other thoughts all raced through Kirk's mind in the half-second it took for Mooch to turn and kneel down at Kirk's side.

Mooch was looking at his cell phone and muttering under his breath. He looked at Kirk, reached toward his face, and lowered his eyelids. Kirk let him. He didn't think he could stop him even if he wanted to.

"Creepy man." Mooch said, and Kirk gathered all his hate and anger. Together, he and his strong anger willed movement. Twitching, Kirk opened his eyes and Mooch started. Kirk had his hands around Mooch's neck and pushed him backward. Mooch yelped like a dog, and Kirk squeezed.

The screams of one Mooch the pooch were muffled as Kirk Weston choked him. Eyes bulging, Kirk pressed his thumbs into Mooch's windpipe and poured all his remaining strength into the choke.

Mooch struggled and kicked, throwing Kirk off balance. He was weak, and everything hurt. He tipped over and landed on his shoulder. It wouldn't have mattered which shoulder, they were both out. He screamed out, but only a guttural grunt escaped.

Mooch was up and on top of Kirk's chest. He swung and hit Kirk across the jaw. One after another, Mooch pounded and punched Kirk in the face. Kirk passed out after the third one landed, and broke his nose. Now he wished he would have stayed dead.

———◦◦◦———

KREIOS DUCKED INTO AN alley. I followed, and the thick crowd of people seemed to open up for the two huge men as they turned to follow us. I ran through all the information I knew about the Brotherhood, but all I could remember was that they were stronger in pairs.

Kreios stopped and turned around, and to my horror, pulled out a short dagger. He was going to fight. Running seemed to be the smart move in this case, but he did not look like he was in the mood to play cat and mouse.

I could feel the all too familiar calm wash over my body, and I let my instincts take over. My heart slowed, and I clenched my hands into fists. If they wanted a fight, I would give them one. I could feel the .9mm strapped to my chest in its holster, but I did not draw. Was I hoping to be killed? Or did I want to fight—was I beginning to crave the battle?

The first man stood a good six-foot-six and had wide shoulders and a fat neck. He grinned, and right before my eyes his skin began to bulge and tear as the demon inside began to tear itself from its shell. I recalled the last encounter, and my heart twisted into a ball. They were getting better at blending in and being able to walk separate of their host. It seemed that they created a shell that was not human but looked the part.

The demon cocked its head back and let out a guttural roar as large black wings unfurled and stretched up and out. They were full of holes and seemed tattered and not of much use, until one came across my chest so fast that I didn't even see it coming.

I tumbled, end over end through the air, and landed on my back, hitting the pavement hard. I could feel the wind whoosh from my lungs, and I forced myself to get up. A bystander turned the corner, screamed, and ran. I jumped to my feet and clenched my fists.

Kreios had his dagger out and pounced on the large beast as the second man rushed me with an ax-looking thing in his hands. He was just as big as the first shell of a man, and had a shock of grey in his black hair. He was quick on his feet, but I was quicker.

I let him come, and as he reached for me, I took a hold of his coat collar, thrust him past me, and tripped him at the same time. He should have gone down, but he somehow stayed on his feet and backhanded me, almost connecting with my exposed jaw. I bent backward and the blow went inches by the tip of my nose.

Kreios and the demon were making the sounds of monster and prey, but I was busy, so I had to trust that he would win.

I squared off with the panting hulk of a man, and he stared me down. I had a feeling that this guy was not used to being out-manned; he did not seem to enjoy missing. I gave him a smile, and that got him going again.

This time he swung and jabbed the ax in a skillful manner, but each blow, I was able to dodge. I could also feel something else. It was some sort of drain; I could feel the energy or life force begin to drain from my body. I at once knew what was going on. This beast was somehow sucking my energy and gaining strength as I grew weaker.

"Kill him quickly, Mark!" Kreios yelled from somewhere behind me. I could feel the strain in his voice, but I could also feel the wave of energy from my core begin to flow outward. I ran toward the end of the alley as my pursuer followed after me. He cursed, and as I turned, my hands were glowing bright white.

Not again. I knew that the last time this happened, I just about blew up an entire building. I did not want to endanger Kreios, but on some other level, I knew he would be fine.

Holstering his ax, the big man turned, picked up a

green dumpster, and raised it above his head. No normal human could be this strong, but somehow this monster had the power of ten men. I wondered if all the Brotherhood could do this.

I charged him, knowing that my core was glowing and my hands were now bright orbs of light. The green, rust-covered dumpster flew through the air, and I slid on my knees bending backward as the metal box flew over my head.

Popping up, I pushed my hands out toward the attacker and willed the energy to move from my hands and into his body. The buildup hurt like fire as a blinding light shot from my hands in a tight stream and slammed into the big man's chest. He screamed and staggered backward, and the flow of energy stopped, but he was still on his feet.

I stepped forward, now only a foot from his sagging form. His coat and undershirt were burnt, and I could see through the skin and into his chest cavity. The bolt of energy had just about gone through him.

I grabbed his head and forced my will to respond. Bright white light consumed my hands, and his head exploded like a melon. I let go, and he dropped to the pavement. A pool of dark blood ran from his carcass and I took one step forward, pulled my .9mm out, and put two in his chest. I was pissed.

Kreios yelled, and I turned to see the demon and Kreios in a hand-to-hand fight to the death.

My body pounded as the energy I used up took its toll. I charged the man who used to hold the winged demon and pulled him off Kreios's back. He had a small dagger buried up to the hilt in Kreios's back.

Kreios almost seemed to be ignoring the man as he struggled with the winged creature. I spun him around and pulled him into a bear hug. He fought against me, but I closed my eyes and let the energy drain from my body.

My hands were wrapped around him and aimed at his back. Searing hot energy burst from my chest and hands, cutting through the man's body. He fell into wet pieces, and I fell with him to the ground.

I sucked in air trying to get more into my lungs. My chest and hands burned, but the light was already fading. So much for my shirt; it had a huge hole in the center and was burned and tattered at the edges.

I pushed myself up to my feet and staggered. Blood and guts covered me from head to foot. I slipped in the mess and almost fell again but managed to stay upright. Kreios let out a yell, and I looked up.

The huge monster bent its legs and took three massive flaps, taking out a fire escape on one side and breaking windows out on the other side of the alley. Kreios was on the demon's back stabbing the beast in the neck with his dagger. The thing let out a yelp and took flight.

I emptied my .9mm into his chest but it didn't seem to faze him. Kreios looked like a little kid riding on a dragon with the size difference. I ran after them as the thing took off farther down the alley. It crashed into a building, tumbled like a Ping-Pong ball, and landed on his back about fifty feet ahead of me.

Running as fast as I could, I looked through the dust and rubble for Kreios. He was gone, and the beast was fighting to turn over. Wings, bent and mangled, worked to right themselves. I loaded my .9mm with a fresh clip and shot him in the forehead.

Pop, pop, pop.

It turned its head and looked at me as if to mock my human efforts. My body was sore, and I felt like some of my strength was returning, but I still felt weak.

I scanned for Kreios but saw nothing. Then, in a blink, Kreios landed feet first on the demon's neck and shattered it with a crunching sound that made me think of a thousand dry sticks. I looked up and then back to Kreios, who was reaching down and taking hold of the two large horns on the broken demon's head. He twisted and yanked the head off and tossed it to the side.

I didn't know what to say, what to think. "So, you fly now?"

Kreios leapt effortlessly to the ground, brushed rubble and dust from his shoulders, and smoothed his garments. "Yes. I learned when I was a boy."

I waited for the rest of the story, but he walked to the overturned dumpster, took some newspaper, and handed it to me. "We need to burn the bodies… now."

"I took the newspaper and it lit as soon as I touched it. I dropped it as once and realized my hands were still hot, but to me, it didn't really burn. He picked up the flaming paper and lit the demon. It went up so fast that I wondered if it fire was its weakness. He took the two other bodies of the men and tossed their pieces into the blaze without saying a word. I just watched, not really knowing what to do.

"We must go."

I nodded. We walked out of the alley and turned past onlookers who glanced into the alley, but the sight of the fire did not slow their progress. It was New York, after all—there are things to do and people to see.

Chapter Thirty

ISIS WATCHED IN HORROR as Kirk flexed his back and let out a guttural scream. It jolted her out of the drug-induced fog. Her hand throbbed, but she pushed it to the back of her mind. Kirk was losing it, and she knew this was it, the moment in every battle where you have that small window to turn the tables. This was that window.

Feet and hands were strapped down, but her captor had made one mistake. After he severed her fingers, he was so focused on Kirk and how he responded that he left the small, rolling metal table next to her. It was just beyond her reach, and she would have to grab a tool with only one finger and a thumb.

The strap on the wounded hand was not as tight because he had had to loosen it in order to pull it away from her body and cut off her fingers. Isis lifted her head and calculated the distance between her hand and the table of sharp tools.

Three inches might as well been three miles. Kirk was thrashing, and she could see blood pouring from his mouth as he bit down on his tongue. *Oh God, what is he doing?* But this was not the time to freak out; she was trained, and now was the time to let that dark part of her take over.

She could remember all the people she had killed, all the horrors they had died for. These memories brought out her evil nature. She was not weak, not just a woman. No, she was one of the most dangerous assassins in the world.

Isis could feel the boils on her face and body, but something was different. She didn't feel bloated anymore. The antidote was working, and her swollen limbs were returning back to normal.

Testing her legs and arms, she noticed that her bonds were looser then even an hour ago. This was good, but her feet would not pull through the padded cuff. But her hands, maybe her hands could slip free in time. But she didn't have time.

Kirk wretched, and the kidnapper stood watching him with clenched fists. He had forgotten about her for the moment.

Isis pushed her hand down into the wet blood and rolled it around, trying to cover her whole hand and wrist. If she were going to get free, it would have to be her wounded hand. It was wet and missing fingers.

Once she had coated her hand as much as she could, Isis looked up at Kirk and forced herself not to scream out. He was vomiting and she could see him bite down on his lip. More blood ran down his chin and he laughed in some other voice. It sent chills up her spine. Her heart broke to see him like this.

It was hard to admit, but she loved him. More than she had ever loved anyone before. She was trained to shut off, to close down her emotions, and Kirk came out of nowhere and tore right through all her defenses. All she wanted was to be with him, to hold him in her arms and make everything okay again. Even if it meant quitting her life with the WJA, she would do it for him.

Now here he was killing himself to save her. He went through hell to get her the antidote, and now she was going to lose him.

No! Not like this… not at the hand of some psycho.

Relaxing her hand, she brought the cuff up and pulled. Her stubs pounded and started bleeding through the rubberized liquid bandages. Twisting a little, she felt it start to slide. She kept her eyes locked on Kirks face, and at once, he threw up and screamed out.

The mirror reflected his face, and when he went limp, Isis pulled with everything she had. Her wrist made a popping sound and came free. Not waiting to look, she took hold of the very knife that took her fingers and gripped it between her remaining finger and thumb.

The knife slipped, and she almost dropped it, but she steadied it and ran it across her other wrist strap. The knife was sharp, so it did not take much pressure, and once her other hand was free, she took the knife in her good hand and cut her feet free.

Her head swam, and every fiber of her body ached and screamed out in protest. She had been drugged, filled with more drugs to counteract the virus, and put through the trauma of losing three fingers, all on top of being stuck on a cold metal table for what seemed like forever.

She stood and stumbled. Gripping the edge of the metal table, she kept from falling. She blew her hair from her eyes, and looked up to see Kirk and the skinny little freak struggling.

Kirk was on the bottom and was being pounded by the masked man. Isis stepped forward, and ran toward the man who was attacking her man.

"Try picking on someone your own size!" Her voice was dry and filled with venom. It hurt to speak, but right now, she couldn't feel much of anything. Her face felt hot, her good hand clutched the fat cleaver, and when the masked man turned at her voice, she was on him.

MOOCH HIT KIRK IN the face once, twice, three times. Kirk was ruining all his plans. He couldn't, for once in his miserable life, play by the rules.

"I hate you! Die, you piece of—" He heard a snap as Kirks nose broke and his head went limp. He knocked him out. *Now who is the man? Not so tough now, are you!*

He was breathing heavily and he looked at his bloody fists. They were shaking.

"Wake, you fool, she is coming."

"Try picking on someone your own size!"

Mooch turned to see Isis rushing toward him and holding the cleaver. He didn't even have enough time to lift his hands in defense. She slashed in a downward swing, and the blade came across his face. He didn't feel anything. She kicked him in the neck, and he tumbled backward.

The concrete floor met his head with a hollow *thud.*

He could smell piss as he voided himself. What was going on? This was all wrong. She was supposed to die, and Kirk was supposed to live a long life consumed by guilt and grief.

He would not go down like this. Struggling to his feet, he swung at nothing and fell on his face. He felt the next blow as Isis hacked him in the back. Mooch grunted and saw a dark shadow cover his vision.

He could see a hole open up. On the edges of this open pit were winged demons and creatures clinging to the sides from roots and the legs of screaming people. He screamed out and tried to clear his vision, but the pit of hell gaped open wider, and he could feel the force of it pull him, suck him in toward the massive maw.

"No, no...*No!*" He clawed backward and was kicked in his ribs. All the air in his lungs burst from his mouth. He tasted the rust flavor of blood, his vision cleared, and he was staring up into the face of the beautiful Isis.

"Any last words, freak?" Her eyes were black and dead. Mooch was scared, and the humming of the stone was dull in his head, like a low rumbling deep in the earth. At once, he knew what it was. It was his mark, the one that would send him to hell.

He tried to speak, to respond, but looking at her made him want to die. She was outlined by a huge bulb giving her a glow that framed her head in a halo. But behind her was some sort of darkness, and he knew that darkness.

She nodded as if reading his mind and came down on him with the bloody cleaver.

CHAPTER THIRTY-ONE

ONE MINUTE, I WAS walking with Kreios, and the next, I couldn't breathe. I sucked in a hard breath, but no air filled my lungs. A firm pressure kept my chest down and kept me from breathing in. I opened my eyes to see a huge man, or was it one of the Brotherhood men, half-demon? He had to be over seven feet tall, and he had one huge hand on my chest holding me down.

He was not looking at me but focused on something else. Beyond us, in a room that looked like a dungeon with low, stone ceilings, and torches instead of electric lights bathed the room in a low orange light.

Clawing at his hand, I tried to pull his fingers back, but it was as if he wasn't there, or maybe… this was a glimpse.

I stopped struggling and found that I was fine—no air needed. But how was I in a glimpse? Was this different from a dream? It seemed that this was a look into the future where a full-on dream could create a new future or reality.

This had to stop.

Focus, Mark. What do you see?

Small room. Three, no, five men. Wooden table in the center—it was a meeting of some sort. They were talking in some other language, not one I could even place. The floor was dirt, so we were underground or in some very old building. I looked up to see if there were cables or plumbing—something to tell me what kind of building we were in.

I couldn't find any pipes or wire, so I looked around again and could feel the glimpse start to fade. The room began to fog over, but at the far end was a door, a large, wooden door with carvings on the face of it. I squinted to try to clear my vision just enough to see what it was, some sort of—

KREIOS LOOKED AT ME standing on the corner of 30th and Lexington as if I was crazy. People moved around us without a second look.

"Are you all right?"

"—Uh, yeah. Just had a …er, I think I just had a glimpse."

"Just now?" He seemed confused, which was not normal for the master of self control.

"Yeah. How long was I out?"

"You were not out at all. You just stopped for a second, and you looked like you were sick." Kreios took my arm and pulled me off to the side so we were not standing right in the middle of the sidewalk. "You mean to tell me that you just had a glimpse? You can dream as you walk?"

"No... I think they are different. I dream when I fall asleep, but most of the time, I wake up out of one. These glimpses can hit at any time and don't steal real time. I don't think they create new worlds, just let me see into the future of the one I am in."

"What did you see? Was the book there?"

"Can't you just read my mind?" I rubbed my hands over my face, pressed my temples, and let the pressure center me.

"No, I can most of the time, but you are blank now—I am getting new thoughts, but it is as though whatever you saw or wherever you were is covered in a shadow." He did not seem happy about this, and seeing this side of him made me feel better. He really didn't know everything or have all the answers. I don't know why this was better than thinking he had all the answers. Maybe I just didn't like feeling lost and alone. At least I knew he was in this with me.

"It was a room, underground, and there were five Brotherhood members—or what looked like them—having a meeting. I couldn't understand what they were saying. It was in some other language."

"Was there anything to give you a time or place? A clock or something dated to see if it was going on now or in the past?"

"No, I think all my glimpses are of the future, so it will happen. I guess I am supposed to find this room. It did have this wooden door. It had these engravings in it..." I patted my pockets, found my keychain sharpie, and drew on my hand. A circle, and in the center was a three point flower-looking thing.

"Like this, or kind of like that, anyway. And all around it were carvings of eagles and a waterfall. Does that mean anything to you?"

I could tell from the look on his face that he knew what the symbol meant. "Yes, it does." He turned and walked across the street. A cab honked at Kreios, and the cabbie swore as he flipped the bird out the window.

"Yo, come on, you can't keep doing this to me!" I ran after Kreios and grabbed him by the shoulder and turned him around. "What? Tell me what you know!"

KIRK ROLLED TO HIS knees and coughed, sending a burst of pain through his ribs and up into the base of his neck. He spit out blood and wiped at his mouth. Isis wrapped her arms around him, and he could smell her hair mixed with salty sweat. It was the best thing he had ever smelled.

"Kirk… are you okay?" Isis held him tight and kissed his neck. His heart felt heavy and at once, he wanted to cry.

"Yeah… you?" He turned his head and looked into her dark eyes. Pools of blackness and mystery. Who was she? Why would she love him; it didn't make any sense. "Your hand—"

"I'll survive."

Kirk sat on the floor, and his senses began to return. The room was hot. He and Isis were soaked in sweat, and both were covered with blood. Some was their own and some of it wasn't. He looked up at Isis and saw tears streaming down her cheeks.

"Come here…" Kirk reached out and brought her to him. He wrapped her in his arms, and she folded into him, and her tiny frame seemed to melt into nothing. She shook as she cried. Kirk ran his hand through her hair and kissed the top of her head.

"It's okay, I'm here, and we're alive. I am so sorry Isis, this is all my fault. He wanted me; I pushed him to this." Kirk's voice cracked, and his swollen tongue made the words hard to say.

Isis turned her face up to him, and with her good hand, stroked the side of his face. "I was so scared, what were you doing to yourself? I thought you were dead, that you were going to kill yourself to keep me alive!"

"Isis—" Her name was all he got out before she pulled his head down to kiss him. Her lips met his, and a shiver rushed down his spine. For a moment there was nothing, no blood, no pain, no fears or memories. Just her lips and his.

She kissed him three times softly. A surge of warmth took over, and he pulled her face to his and pressed hard, kissing her hungrily. She responded with just as much force, and time seemed to stop. For once in his life, something was the way it should be.

"I love you, Isis—" His voice was gruff, and his words meshed into one word. "I-love-you-Isis."

"I love you, too, Kirk… I love you so much!" Kirk smiled at her, kissed her on one cheek, and then on the other, taking away her tears.

"Isis, I fell for you the first time I saw you. I tried to

fight it, but I can't get you out of my head." She smiled at him and nodded.

"I know. Me too. Thanks for saving my life."

Kirk laughed. "You too!"

A scraping sound of metal on concrete brought Kirk's eyes past Isis, and before he could react, Isis's body jerked at the same instant Kirk heard the gunshot.

CHAPTER THIRTY-TWO

KREIOS SPUN AROUND AS I turned him, and his eyes flashed. "I do not have the time to explain this to you! I am here, trying to save your life, and it is plain to see that we will not only not find the book in time, but you get captured by the Brotherhood."

"Hey, calm down." Kreios was shaking and seemed about to lose it, and I did not want to be around when he lost his temper. "I'm trying. I don't know what you want or what to do. If I have to go and kill my other selves to keep this thing from going crazy, I will do it. But I don't know how to not dream, I don't know how to stop all of this outside of changing it in my book so that I'll be unable to dream."

"If we do not find the book, then you will keep creating worlds, and I am out of time. This attack on us is just the beginning. You will be hunted through time and in every dimension."

"You tell me, Kreios, where is this book? What does the symbol mean? You know something."

Kreios sighed, turned, and walked away. I followed and walked next to him as we headed toward Brooklyn.

"I was given six days. We are out of time, Mark. I have no choice but to kill you. If you die, the rest go with you. It is the simplest way to re-adjust things. I am sorry, truly, I am."

I stopped and stared at him. This had to be wrong, there had to be another way. I was not going to just lie down without a fight. I wanted to live, to be with K and Sam. I knew now what I really wanted, and it was K. She was always the one, the first and only to make me complete.

"You are just going to kill me? We can fight them together. You saw how we beat them. Let them come, and we will do the same to all the Brotherhood. You have to give me another chance!"

"No, Mark, there is no more time. That was just two. Next time, it will be four, and six and a host, until you and I are both dead. I will let you say goodbye to K and Sam, but that is the extent of what I can do. I am sorry."

This couldn't be it. I thought of the WJA. Could I get everyone together, stand, and fight? Then we could hold them off, maybe all look for the book and find it quicker. But how could I when I was the only one who could go from one world to another?

"You said the book was here, in this world. We are so close… Why are you giving up now?" It didn't make any sense.

"I was wrong. Your mind is broken, taking you to

random places where you have unfinished business. I do not know what you need to do here, but that room you saw, that symbol is only found in the realm."

"The realm? Where is that?"

Not on this earth, and it is not somewhere you can go if you are alive. If you were there or are going to go there, you must be dead. One more reason that I have to kill you, Mark. It may be the only way for you to find the book and maybe fix all this."

"But it won't matter. When I die, it is all over, anyway. What is the point?"

"I do not know. Even I do not know all the answers."

This was it, the end of my luck. I survived so many things and had these abilities that I couldn't explain, and I knew that I was connected to Kreios somehow, but there was no outrunning my own fate.

"Take me home, Kreios. I need to see my family."

ISIS GASPED AND LOOKED into Kirk's eyes. The spark that hid in the darkness flickered, and she mouthed something. Kirk pleaded with her with his eyes. *No, please, no!*

"I love you… Kirk Weston." It was a whisper but clear. She reached up, pulled him to her, and kissed him. Her lips were wet, and he felt her body tense and release.

"I love you, Isis, more then you will ever understand." Kirk held her tight, but she was gone. Body limp and no movement or breath on his neck. With eyes closed, he let the moment soak into his mind. He would not forget, never forget this.

"Now you know, Kirk Weston! You know what it feels like to have the one you love ripped from you! I hate you, Weston. I hope you suffer for the rest of your life!"

Mooch gurgled, laughed, and struggled to his feet. Blood gushed from his neck where Isis cut his throat. He clutched a .45 in his right hand.

Kirk laid Isis down gently and stood up. His head swam, and he just about fell over as the room spun. He was beyond angry, past rage, and all he knew was that Mooch was going to die.

"Don't move, Kirk Weston." Mooch raised the gun and leveled it at Kirk. "I will kill you, but I don't want to. I want you to live a long and miserable life and suffer for what you did."

Kirk stepped toward Mooch and clenched his fists. "Go on, Mooch, shoot me. I am going to kill you, so you better kill me if you want to live."

"I am dead already. You killed me once, but I lived. You can't kill me again; he won't let me die. We are invincible!"

Kirk looked at Mooch, who was grinning like a demon. Mustering his remaining strength, he charged Mooch.

"I told you—" Mooch fired twice but Kirk didn't stop.

Hitting Mooch in the chest with his shoulder, they both went down to the concrete. Kirk landed on top and pushed himself up as the gun went skittering across the floor. Mooch grunted and lost hold of his neck. Blood poured from the large gash across his throat.

"You killed her! You killed her!" Kirk was screaming and crying as he punched Mooch in the face. It was like punching a wet sack of golf balls. He did not feel his hand break, did not feel his broken ribs or the two bullet holes in his left lung. He was going to kill Mooch, and that was that.

Mooch was laughing, blood splattering left and right with each blow, spraying a pattern on the concrete floor. The sound of him laughing made Kirk hit harder.

Mooch coughed and tried to fight back, but Kirk would not let up. His laugh turned into a bubbly scream. Fear filled his smashed face, and Kirk stopped when Mooch's head went limp. He had passed out or was dead, but he was not dead enough. Not dead enough for what he did.

Kirk crawled after the gun and took it, checked the clip and slammed it back into place. Standing up, Kirk dragged himself over to Mooch's body. He kicked him in the ribs, and Mooch woke with a start. He rolled over on his side, coughing up blood.

"Time for you to die, and this time I am doing it on purpose. Rot in hell!"

Mooch turned to look through swollen eyes at Kirk. "No!"

Pop.

Pop.

Pop.

Pop.

Pop.

Pop.

Pop. Kirk shot Mooch in the head, not messing with the body. He didn't want to see his face ever again. Blood and brain twisted into each other, and Mooch lay on the floor looking more like a movie prop then a person.

Kirk went over to the small rolling table and took the

biggest knife he could find. After cutting the head free, as well as all Mooch's limbs, he found gasoline and lit the body on fire. He knew he was dying and would not make it much longer. His breathing was raspy and wet. With the hospitals full from virus victims, he was already too far gone to be helped.

Sitting down on the floor, he watched the body of his friend burn. He held Isis and cried. Stroking her hair, he kissed her one last time and closed his eyes.

He thought of his life, of his failed marriage. How he was so cruel to his wife and how he didn't blame her for leaving him. He was a jerk and was constantly in a foul mood. Then, the case that changed his life forever. David's Island, and the inmates all dying of poisoning. It led him to the WJA and to Isis. He thought of her, and how he would melt when she talked. How she saw past his mask and saw something different in him. She loved him, and that was enough, he was happy. Imagine that, he was a happy man, knowing he and his love would be together somewhere beyond. He was loved.

"Goodnight, baby, I'll see you soon."

CHAPTER THIRTY-THREE

K STOOD ON THE back porch, looking at Sam play in the sandbox. I came up behind her and kissed the side of her neck. She sighed and turned to kiss me. I drank in her lips and skin, knowing that I would not see or feel them again. This was the end, but for her I was still me and would come home just like always. I couldn't tell her that I was already dead.

"Hey, babe." She smiled and her eyes sparkled.

"Hey, you look amazing."

"Aw, thanks, you charmer. I bet you say that to all the girls."

"Want to sit?" I led her to the porch swing.

"Sure, Sam and I read books all day. Not much else to do with no power and all." The thought of them being alone through this collapse made me sick inside. But if I stayed, I risked the chance that the Brotherhood would kill them to get to me.

"That's good, she likes reading. I bet she will be a writer one day. Wouldn't that be cool, to have a writer in the family?"

"Yeah, she is smart. A little too smart for her own good, though." K giggled and leaned her head on my shoulder. "What's going on, Mark? The virus? The agency? I have been so scared for you and everyone."

"It's all going to be fine. It will all work out. I am just glad you and Sam didn't get sick."

"I've been watching her, and she seems normal. I was freaking out after you called."

"All that matters is I am here now. We are safe and together. I don't know what is going to happen, but I know we will be fine."

"Good, I kind of like you."

"I kind of like you, too."

I wrapped my fingers in with K's and kissed each one. She looked at me and smiled. "You know how I like that. What are you trying to do to me?"

"I just miss you, I feel like I haven't seen you in such a long time. I just want to remember you, like this. Happy and safe."

"Remember? Are you going to go away again?"

"Yes, I have to go overseas, and I don't know how long I will be gone. It has to be done and will do a lot to fix the mess we're in. Our futures and the future of this country depend on this. But with all that is going on, it is risky… do you understand?"

"You may not come home."

I nodded. "I love you, K, always have."

"I love you, too, Mark. You are my one and only." I

kissed her. We held each other and watched Sam play.

———⁕———

I HELD IT TOGETHER until I left the house. K and Sam were in bed, and I slipped out so I didn't have to say goodbye. I couldn't do it. I had to talk Kreios out of this, to at least try to fight.

"No, Mark." Kreios stepped out from the shadows and stepped in front of me. "If there were any other way, or if we had more time…"

I stepped off the curb and began to walk down the street. I looked back to my house, the house K and I bought after we were married. I felt a lump grow in my throat, and I turned to Kreios.

"I don't want to die, Kreios. I want to stay and fight. I feel like this is giving up."

"It is not giving up. This is the only way. You die to save your life, you die to save your family. Or will you sacrifice them so you can live?"

"There has to be another way!" I was not going to go down like this. My entire life, I fought. I was not just going to let someone kill me when there was still a chance.

Kreios took my arm, and I wrenched it away, my hands glowing with energy.

"Mark, stop."

"No, there has to be another way, I won't let you just kill me."

"Then you leave me no choice." Kreios grabbed me and shot up into the air. We flew straight up, and I struggled to get free of his grip, but he was like iron. My hands were hot, and I could feel energy flow through my arms and legs.

"Let me go!"

Kreios took me by the arms and held me out from his body. "Mark, do not make this harder than it has to be. You will not win." He tossed me, and I tumbled end over end. I was unaware of where I was or what end was up, only that I was falling, and falling fast.

I saw building and brick flash before my eyes just before I hit. I slammed to a stop and shook my head, trying to clear my vision. Kreios landed so fast that the rooftop shook. I looked at him and got to my feet.

We stood on top of a building, but I didn't know where or how far he had thrown me.

"I will fight you, Kreios. You are not the only one with abilities."

I flipped my wrist and brought both my hands together. A bright, white light shot from them and hit Kreios dead in the chest. Kreios slid backward and rushed me so fast that his body was just a blur.

I jumped up, and he flew under me, but turned before I could land. He took my foot and yanked me down. I hit hard, and I tasted blood in my mouth. I rolled, and light consumed my body. Some was from Kreios, but most was from me. I watched as he took hold of my shoulders and punched me in the face.

The blow felt like raw steel. I fell backward but managed to stay upright. Kreios was shirtless as my energy burned off his clothing. He was pure muscle, and his skin was bright white. Tattoos winding up his arms and neck glowed hot yellow. I began to regret my decision to fight him. He was not of this earth, and I was… well, who knew what I was.

I looked at my hands, and my head pounded with a sharp pain right behind my eyes. "Stand down, Kreios."

Kreios didn't answer, just stepped forward. I reached for him and let all the energy flow from my body. Kreios disappeared in the bright light flowing from my body. I was the human bomb once again. I remembered how it felt when I stood against the Red Dog.

A pulse pounded from my body and sent a shockwave out in a circle around me. I collapsed to the rooftop, grabbed my ears, and pulled at them. They must have burst, because I couldn't hear anything but a low hum.

I sucked in air and opened my eyes. Kreios stood over me, glowing with the same energy I had. His eyes burned, and he was now naked. I could see raw muscle and bone all over his body. I had hurt him, but not nearly enough to kill him; he was healing as I stared at him.

"I am sorry, Mark. You are a good man, but it is time." I couldn't hear him, but he was in my thoughts, I could hear him in my head. He reached down and placed his hands on each side of my head. I felt pressure fill my brain, and I clamped my eyes shut. White light took over and the silence… was…

CHAPTER THIRTY-FOUR

BEEP, BEEP, BEEP, BEEP...

Shhhhhh-kuh, shhhhhh-kuh, beep, beep, beep...

Tick, tock, tick, tock...

Beep, beep, beep...

I opened my eyes and saw bright, white light. My eyes hurt. Was I supposed to have pain up here, or wherever I was? Where was I?

I blinked and opened my eyes again, and saw that it was not a room of light, but just a light. Two bulbs in two rows and covered with a plastic cover. I tried to turn my head, but couldn't.

Beep, beep, beep...

I could feel my fingers, as if new blood was flowing for the first time. They tingled, and I tried to lift my arms, but again couldn't move.

Shhhhhh-kuh, shhhhhh-kuh, beep, beep, beep...

I had something in my mouth, down my throat—a tube

or something. I almost gagged, but forced myself to relax. A few minutes went by, and I managed to move my head a little. I was in a room, most likely a hospital. Had I won? Did Kreios fail to kill me?

A heart monitor made beeping sounds, and next to that was what looked like a breathing machine. The screen to the heart rate monitor had a logo in the top center. I blinked and squinted trying to read the tiny letters.

W. J. A.

My mind raced to remember where I was, when I was, and how I survived. WJA. I know what it meant but did not want to know. It wasn't that simple, not that... couldn't be. I fought Kreios. I had lived and somehow was here, wherever here was.

Tick, tock, tick, tock...

All the sounds in the room seemed amplified, and I wondered if it was because of my eardrums bursting. How could I still hear? I found the clock; it was on the wall down past my feet. It was a boring thing, a black frame with a white background. Just below the center of the clock was a label. It read, *"Solomon Timepiece."*

Where was I? What was going on? I had been... where? The memory was like a dream. Once I woke up, it was fading fast. Had I been asleep?

I knew... I knew what it was, all of it. For one second, I knew what it was. I was here. Here is the now, this was me, and this was real. Kreios, who was he? What was he?

A click, and the door opened. A tall black man entered the room wearing blue scrubs. He looked at me, and did a double take.

"Mr. Appleton?" He rushed to me, took out a light, and

flashed it into my eyes. It was that same white light, the energy I knew so well, the same light.

The man looked from screen to screen and smiled. "Mr. Appleton, can you hear me? If you can, blink twice."

I blinked twice, and he clapped his hands. "Great." He seemed overjoyed.

I tried to move again, but could only move my fingers a little and my head a little more. I looked the man over as he checked me and the machines that were keeping me alive.

"Mr. Appleton, you have been in a coma. Do you remember anything?"

I blinked once—I figured that was the code for, "No."

He nodded and smiled. You were in an accident four years ago. You have been in a coma and non-responsive. You are one lucky man." Leaving the room, he returned a few minutes later with a woman in a long white robe.

The doctor looked me over and flashed the light in my eyes again. I was now able to move my head and my hand a little more. It took some time, but they took the tube out of my mouth, and I sucked in fresh air, which burned like fire.

"Now don't try to speak, Mr. Appleton. You have not used your voice in some time and we don't want to overdo it. I am Doctor Weston, and this is Kirk." She pointed to the black man, who smiled.

"We did not have much hope for you to pull out of this, but I do believe we have witnessed a miracle."

This was all wrong. I tuned out the rest of what they said. Kirk, he was the nurse assigned to me. The doctor, the clock, the WJA. It was all here. My brain took things and put them together to make another world. My heart sank, and I felt like throwing up. A panic took over, and I began to breathe fast and deep. I couldn't get enough air.

"Calm down, Mr. Appleton. Take it easy, breathe slow and deep." Doctor Weston took my hand and said, "Do you remember the accident?"

I blinked once.

"Four years ago, you were in an explosion at the Super Mart. Do you remember that?"

No, not again. It wasn't true, couldn't be. Why was this happening to me? Tears filled my eyes and, she leaned over to wipe them away.

"It is hard, I know. I am so sorry Mr.—Mark. You survived, but broke your back. I am sorry, but you are paralyzed from the waist down." I looked up at her in shock. I couldn't be paralyzed; I could feel my feet, I could feel my legs, and they hurt.

I blinked fast, and she looked to Kirk and the other two nurses. "Bring me some water, please." Kirk left the room and returned with some water in a plastic cup and a bendy straw.

I took a drink. It felt good and hurt all at the same time.

"Mark, I know that this is hard, and I don't want to be the one to tell you, but you will find out eventually." I knew what she was going to say. I knew but didn't want to hear it, couldn't.

"Your wife and daughter were with you, they didn't make it. I am so sorry, Mark. My heart breaks for you." Doctor Weston cried and held onto my hand as I sobbed. It was too much for me to take. I couldn't do this anymore.

I just wanted to die, to really die so I didn't have to be thrown into real and fake worlds, to just be at rest. But more than that, I wanted K, I wanted Sam, I wanted to hold them, I wanted to kiss my wife, and I wanted to hold her again.

After a time, I opened my eyes and was alone again. I could see the sun streaming in through the window. I knew now that it was all a dream. A dream in a dream, or my mind trying to keep me alive, pulling from things and people around me to create this other world. Was that what other coma patients went through? If they never pulled out of it or realized it was just a dream, they would be in a coma for life. Trapped inside of their own heads.

But was that a bad thing? I could live a full life in my dreams. I could hold K and Sam; I could love Maria and my son. Was it the inner desires that created it all? Could it be controlled?

I wiggled my toes and knew that I was going to walk again. I would live and might even have a chance to be happy. The dream was fading and almost gone from me now. Memories I had were now just feelings, but I feared that if I let them go, I would be lost forever.

How could I let K go? I knew how to keep her, how to keep Sam, Maria, and everyone I loved. I knew how to live with them. This life is the people you love. I didn't want to live without them, even if in a fake, made up world in my dreams.

It was better to dream with them than to live without them.

I closed my eyes and called up my memories. Let them take me away into my dreams. In my dreams, I was a father, a husband, and a hero. It was real, this life is the sham, the fake mask hiding what is down deep. I would see K again, I would hold and play with Sam. I would live in my dreams.

Epilogue

A WOMAN STOOD LOOKING through the glass window of Mark Appleton's room. She watched him cry and now fall asleep. She had dark skin like coffee and cream. Her smooth black hair reflected the fluorescent lights above.

Isis was beautiful and dangerous.

Flipping open her cell, she waited for an answer. After three rings, he picked up.

"He's awake."

THE END

AUTHORS NOTE:

I WANT TO THANK you for reading this series. I know that for many of you, this was way out of the box, and I applaud you for sticking in there with me. Even though this is a cross-genre series, which I know is against the rules, I figure the rules are meant to be broken.

I dreamed the first book idea, and each plot in each book came to me as I slept, so you see how I have dreams as the theme. I want to say first that this came from me. I knew from the beginning where the series was going to go, so from the first turn to this ending, all were meant to be just as they are. Now, the story along the way just did its own thing, and I had no idea how supernatural it would get, but that is the fun of writing.

Ideas like the WJA and the tube that ran under the ground came from the bank tubes you and I use every week. The weapons all came from my contacts in the FBI and military and are based on real weapons that are being created. I took some creative liberties, of course.

The abilities Mark has are from my teen series, *Airel*. He and Kreios are a crossover from that series, and in fact, I wrote *Airel* based on parts of the Mark Appleton series.

I hope you had as much fun as I did and look for other Mark Appleton books that will be outside of this series. I even have a Solomon book in the works about how he started the WJA. We will see where my mind takes me.

Thanks again for reading.

August 11, 2011
Boise, Idaho
Aaron Patterson

Made in the USA
Lexington, KY
23 August 2012